STAR CROSSED

Other books by Jane McBride Choate:

Think of Me
Convincing David
Heartsong Lullaby
Never Too Late for Christmas
Mile-High Love
Cheyenne's Warrior Rainbow
Desert Paintbox

STAR CROSSED

•

Jane McBride Choate

AVALON BOOKS
NEW YORK

Published by Thomas Bouregy & Co., Inc.
160 Madison Avenue, New York, NY 10016

Library of Congress Cataloging-in-Publication Data

Choate, Jane McBride.
    Star crossed / Jane McBride Choate.
        p. cm.
    ISBN 978-0-8034-9863-1 (acid-free paper)
    1. Actresses—Fiction.   I. Title.
    PS3553.H575S73 2007
    813'.54—dc22

                                2007024154

PRINTED IN THE UNITED STATES OF AMERICA
ON ACID-FREE PAPER
BY HADDON CRAFTSMEN, BLOOMSBURG, PENNSYLVANIA

To my sister Carla. Together, we can do anything.

Chapter One

Sharp pain sliced between her eyes as she squinted against the glare of the sun bouncing off the car window.

The two or three days Star spent on the road would do her good, she decided—give her time to put her career, her life, in perspective. The drive to her home in Los Angeles was just the ticket to line up her thoughts in some kind of organized manner.

She liked tooling along in the little red rental car over the deserted ribbon of Wyoming highway. She saw a sign announcing the Continental Divide and took a moment to wonder if it was a guidepost for her own life.

Was it time to divide herself from the path she'd chosen to include more in what was seeming a very empty life? She switched off the car radio, preferring to steep

1

herself in the silence. Noise defined and consumed too much of her existence. The quiet was a benediction, an opportunity to listen to the inner voice that was too frequently drowned out by the demands of others.

The landscape slid by, bleached and battered by the savagery of the sun. Not a cloud in sight. She was seeing firsthand the effects of the drought that had made the headlines.

Star Whitney had played the female lead in a dozen westerns. Yet she'd never understood the devastation heat and sun could wreak upon the land. Until now.

What kind of people made their living from such a desolate land, she wondered. And what did it do to their spirits, their souls, when they saw their dreams dry up and blow away with the wind?

Such meanderings were uncharacteristic, she supposed, for a woman who made her living fulfilling the public's desire for fantasy.

An actress, she was supposed to adhere to certain standards. She flouted them easier than she had the strictures her grandmother had foisted upon her when she'd been a child.

She liked what she did and knew she was good at it. It was a liberating feeling, letting her ride out the rough bumps of a career dependent upon the whims of a fickle public. She'd paid her dues, working her way up from walk-ons to where she was today.

Star had no false modesty about her talent. She had made it to the top and, more important, managed to hang on to that spot, but it no longer gave her the satisfaction it once had. She could take her pick and name her own price. Another movie. A television offer. Even a shot at a Broadway play.

But the spark was missing.

The demands of her schedule began to crowd her mind, and she closed her eyes, determined to push away all thought of her obligations, at least for the length of the trip. Every moment of her life felt pinched, and she was beginning to resent the commitments of her career. She could almost hear the clank of bars snapping shut on her.

Not a good sign.

She'd begged her agent for a role that demanded she reach inside herself, to find the grit and guts she knew she could bring to a part.

Her career had been built upon fluff pieces, not that she had anything against the romantic westerns that had made her a star. She knew they had their place, but so did the more serious work that pulled at her.

She had it in her to do more substantial parts, movies that touched hearts, lives.

Months ago, she'd put a bug in her agent's ear about finding her a different kind of role.

"You don't need the money," Brian had said. "You're the top female box office draw. Why take a chance on something that might not be right for you?"

Brian had been right about her not needing the money, but there was more to life than money. There was satisfaction from facing a challenge and meeting it. There was testing herself and stretching her talent. She wanted a chance to discover for herself just what she could do. Still, she'd been content to let him guide her career, trusting in his judgment.

Stick with what you know, he'd told her. Don't rock the boat. Why knock a good thing? He'd used every cliche there was. And because he was good at his job, and, more because he was a friend, she'd let him get away with it.

Until she'd discovered that Brian had turned away the kind of meaty part she'd been hungry to try. She'd walked out without waiting to hear his excuses. They'd talk, she thought, when she reached LA. When her brain, and not her temper, was in control. Right now, she needed time to herself, for herself.

"Don't send out search parties," she'd told him. "I deserve a break and I'm taking it. Cancel the talk show appearance. There's nothing else that can't wait."

"What about that TV project I told you about? Don't you want to at least look at it?"

"When I get back. Maybe. If I'm still speaking to you."

"How can I reach you?"

She heard the pout in his voice. "You can't."

"What about the shoot?"

The publicity shoot, taken on location, had brought her to this spot in Wyoming.

"You have enough photos to plaster my picture over

most of western civilization." Relenting, she touched his hand briefly. "Don't worry about me. I need some time to think."

That was why she was driving to LA instead of taking the plane. That was why her foot was a bit too heavy on the accelerator. That was why she wasn't paying attention to the rabbit that darted across the road in a blur of brown.

She swerved and let out a breath when she avoided hitting the animal. Her relief died abruptly when the car kept going right over the side of the road, coming to a halt only when it rested in a deep gully in a wave of dust. She slumped over the steering wheel, until her heartbeat slowed to a normal pace.

When she felt steady enough, she turned on the ignition. Steam—or was it smoke?—billowed from the engine. She undid the seatbelt and scrambled from the car.

Images of exploding cars on television dramas rushed through her mind. When no eruption followed, it seemed anti-climatic. The hiss escaping her lips was one of relief mingled with exasperation for her runaway imagination.

She shaded her eyes and tried to see beyond the haze of heat and sand. Nothing moved. Not even a breeze gave relief to the overwhelming heat.

The sheer vastness of the high desert filled her with awe. And terror. She knew nothing about survival in such a land. She had only a bottle of water and a suitcase full of pretty clothes. She did the only thing she could. She climbed back inside the car and began tapping on the horn.

Rafe Mackenzie scanned the horizon, looking for the source of the distress signal he'd heard. It had been faint but persistent until a few minutes ago when the sound had died.

He snatched off his hat and swiped at his face with his bandanna. Heat rolled over him, rolled through him. The drought had wrung the life from the land, and from his heart.

If he didn't make it through this season, he feared there wouldn't be a next. That was why he was driving his herd to the high country, before the season, trying to save them.

A roundup. It was something out of the nineteenth century, a tradition that hadn't died. Breeding by artificial insemination rather than nature's way, bottom lines and profit margins, all had taken their toll on the tradition of ranching that his ancestors had cherished.

But the roundup had survived. Participating in one never failed to restore Rafe's spirits, though he had little reason to rejoice otherwise. The Heartsong Ranch, in his family for five generations, was perilously close to bankruptcy.

Beef prices had plummeted in the last decade as Americans grew more health-conscious and treated beef like poison.

At one time, the uncharacteristic pessimism would have worried him. It wasn't his nature to look on the darker side of life. Lately, though, that's all he'd been able to see.

He caught a glimpse of color. The dun-tinted landscape didn't boast any color but brown and more brown, definitely not the gleaming red that caught his eye. He touched his heels to his mount's flanks.

Bear gave a sharp whinny. His powerful legs ate up the distance with ease. When the ground grew too rough, Rafe dismounted and walked the rest of the way. He wouldn't risk Bear. The big gelding had been with him nearly as long as he could sit a horse.

He hiked down the gully and stopped.

A fancy sports car—small, sleek, and glossy—lay slumped there, as though taking a nap. He gave the car a dismissive look. It didn't belong in the middle of southern Wyoming.

A woman was tucked in behind the steering wheel. Hair the color of obsidian obscured her face. The slash of cheekbones was strong, a pretty contrast to the soft, full mouth. Her gold skin was pink with the beginnings of sunburn. He leaned over her, finding the pulse at the base of her neck, reassured to find it strong and steady.

He took a moment to study her. A city girl, judging by her clothes. Only a city girl would tackle these rough and ready roads with a low-slung toy like the red convertible. He did a quick check of the car's interior and found an empty water bottle.

He gave a disgusted snort. Impractical clothing, no water, and a car more suited to city streets than unpaved roads. The only sensible thing she appeared to have done was to tap out the distress signal on the horn. He shook her.

She awoke slowly, lifted her arms, stretching in a way that had him wetting his lips. Spellbound by the most beautiful face he'd ever seen, he forgot to breathe.

Wide eyes grew wider as they registered his presence. She looked about as skittish as a just-birthed foal. He felt her tense under his hands.

He backed off slightly. "Don't worry. I'm just checking for broken bones."

She relaxed fractionally, though her eyes were wary.

He kept his voice low, non-threatening. "Relax. I'm not going to hurt you." Her scent, fresh as a field of wildflowers, stirred his senses. "Are you hurt?"

She grimaced. "My shoulder. I hit it on the steering wheel."

He ran his hands over her. "I don't think it's broken. Probably bruised it up real good."

He continued to probe her shoulder, but his eyes were on her face. She was beautiful. Maybe she was an angel, plopped here in the middle of the high plains of Wyoming to take his mind off his ever present problems.

"Take it easy," she said.

"What? Oh, sorry." He'd been so caught up in the fathomless depths of her blue eyes that he hadn't realized he was still probing the delicate bones.

He felt his pulse thud as his gaze shifted to take in her pale gold skin and full lips. He couldn't remember the last time he had experienced such a sharp tug of attraction. Ruthlessly, he tamped it down. His response to her was immediate and totally unwanted.

He opened his canteen and handed it to her. She took a long drink. "Easy," he cautioned. "Not too much at once."

He helped her from the car, holding on to her until he was sure she could stand by herself. Her mouth, soft and unpainted, trembled slightly.

To distract himself from that image, he flipped the latch on the hood of the snazzy car and looked inside. Ranching made a man a jack of all trades, and he'd had enough experience with engines to recognize this one wasn't going anywhere.

He turned back to her. "How'd you wind up like this?"

Her pretty lips bowed up in a smile. "I swerved to avoid hitting a rabbit."

"You did this"—he gestured to the crumpled car—"so you wouldn't hit Bugs Bunny?"

Her smile turned sheepish.

He gave a low whistle. "Lady, you're either crazy about rabbits or just plain crazy."

She didn't like that. The narrowing of her eyes proved that. Well, that was okay by him. He'd always figured plain speaking was the best way to get the facts across. Truth be told, he didn't know any other way.

"The names's Star," she said sharply. "Star Whitney." She appeared to wait for some sign of recognition.

"Pleased to meet you, Star Whitney. Rafe Mackenzie."

"Mr. Mackenzie."

"Rafe."

Her hand felt fine-boned, small in his. She was tall, nearly five-nine or ten, he guessed, but she looked fragile enough to be blown away by a strong wind. She probably starved herself to get that reed-thin figure.

The sleek car was as out of place as her high-heeled boots and silk blouse.

"If you're finished staring, maybe you can tell me what we're going to do about this."

He slammed the hood shut and retrieved her suitcase from the back seat. He opened it, gave a rueful look at the contents, and tossed it back. Full of city clothes that wouldn't last a day in the middle of the high country.

Her chin raised a fraction of an inch. "You can't just leave me here."

"Don't plan on it."

"What do you plan to do?" Her voice was green-apple tart, and he felt a grin pulling at his lips.

He'd known her less than five minutes and already he was noticing that she was irritating, bossy, and thoroughly annoying. He sighed. Trouble seemed to stick to him like white on rice.

She tapped her foot. "Well?"

"I'm taking you with me." She was going to be trouble. He felt it as surely as he did the energy-sapping heat. A smart man didn't go looking for trouble, but neither did he walk away from someone who needed him. At least, Sam Mackenzie's son didn't.

Rafe had learned early on that Mackenzies did what they could to help out others—neighbor, friend, stranger, it didn't matter. Taking Star Whitney with him was not a wise choice. It was the only choice.

"Mr. Mackenzie—"

"Rafe."

She used her hands when she talked, gesturing with them in a way that told him it was habitual with her.

She was wheedling. He was dismayed to find he was susceptible to blue eyes and pale gold skin. In the sunlight, her dark hair showed hints of red, making him long to sift his fingers through it.

"It's you who doesn't understand," he said. "I have a thousand head to get to water before they die."

He started off at a brisk pace. He needed to get back. The others would be waiting for him.

She trotted after him gamely. She had spunk. He'd give her that. And, unless he missed his guess, a fair share of pride that prevented her from asking for help.

He understood pride, respected it, even when it was misplaced.

"How much farther?" she asked.

He stopped. "A mite."

By the time they reached the spot where he'd tethered Bear, she was panting heavily.

"This is Bear."

She eyed him warily. "He's very big."

Rafe nearly smiled. Big. That was all she could say about the best cutting horse this side of the Colorado River?

He climbed astride, then pulled her up and settled her in front of him.

They made the trip back to camp in less than thirty minutes, every one of them spent with her settled against him.

"Where are we?" Star asked when they reached camp.

"Camp."

"Camp what?"

"Honey, this is camp." He gestured to the men hunkered around the fire.

"Don't call me honey." Her voice took on an edge and she tossed her hair back.

The faintest of smiles flitted around his mouth. "What should I call you?"

"Look, I'll give you whatever you want if you'll just get me to somewhere with a phone." At his blank look, she elaborated. "You know, civilization."

He scratched his head, a gesture she felt sure was more contrived than genuine. "Well, princess, I never thought civilization was all it was cracked up to be."

She scowled. "Princess?"

He gave her an innocent look. "You said not to call you honey." He traced a finger between her brows where lines had formed. "You'll get wrinkles if you frown like that."

That served to deepen her frown.

"Even a princess looks prettier when she smiles." He grinned suddenly, an engaging one that made him look abruptly younger.

She didn't need this. Her chin jutted out, and she squared her shoulders, determined to show him that she wasn't the fluff-brained bimbo he thought.

"You look mighty cute when you stick your chin out like that, princess."

She didn't call him on the ridiculous name this time; she'd be darned if she'd give him the satisfaction. He just wanted to get a rise out of her.

The breath whooshed from her on a sign of frustration.

She couldn't stay angry with him. Especially when she needed him, and need him she did. There was something about him that said things would be on his terms or not at all.

"The name's Star."

He touched two fingers to the brim of his hat. "I'll remember."

She took a deep breath and admitted what was really bothering her. She was flummoxed by her reaction to him.

It annoyed her how far back she had to tip her head to meet his gaze. At five-feet-nine inches, she wasn't accustomed to people towering over her, but Rafe topped her by a good six inches. His chambray shirt was darkened with perspiration, the sleeves rolled up to reveal arms ropey with muscle and sinew. Sunlight caught the sheen of sweat that glossed his skin.

She was accustomed to good-looking men and knew it wasn't the physical package that made him so compelling. She'd starred opposite most of the current leading men in Hollywood, heartthrobs all of them. None of them came close to equaling the aura this man gave off so effortlessly.

His eyes were steady and clear, radiating integrity and strength. Whatever misgivings she felt about being alone with him vanished under the unwavering gaze he leveled at her.

She felt out of place in her silk blouse and designer jeans, but she didn't intend on apologizing for what couldn't be helped. She had never seen the sense in it.

The cock of his chin, the thumbs hooked in his belt, the way his weight was balanced on the balls of his feet, all made her think of a gunslinger from a B western ready to take on the bad guys. Deliberately, she mimicked his pose. She'd stared down hard-nosed producers with nothing more than a haughty look. One dark-eyed cowboy wasn't going to frighten her.

"Well, cowboy, what're we going to do?"

"I've got a roundup to finish. And seeing as I'm stuck with you, you get to come with me."

The idea was ludicrous. She didn't have time to mosey across the country with a bunch of cows. She had obligations, commitments, people who were counting on her. She had a life.

"Take me somewhere I can catch a plane to LA. I'll pay you." She reached for her purse.

His laugh was irritatingly amused. "Look around you. We're in the middle of nowhere." He pointed in the direction of the mountains. "I don't have time for taking you anywhere."

Her gaze settled on the expanse of prairie—beautiful and desolate and altogether frightening to a city-bred girl. Still, she had obligations. "Loan me a horse, point me in the right direction, and I'll get out of your way."

"I can't do that. What do you do in LA that's so all-fired important?"

"I'm in . . . the media." She struggled, but couldn't free her hand. "You have no right to keep me here."

"I've got every right. I'm responsible for you."

"No one even knows I'm here."

"I don't care what the rest of the world thinks. It's myself I have to answer to."

She looked at him, really looked, and saw what she'd failed to understand before. He was a man you could count on. He didn't care what others thought. His own honor was all that mattered. It was a concept too frequently missing in the circles she moved in.

He rummaged through a saddlebag and tossed her some clothes. "Try these. They belong to Johnny. He's not much bigger than you. They ought to fit."

"I don't wear other people's clothes."

"I'm sorry. We don't run to many Rodeo Drive boutiques out here."

"You don't—" She'd been about to explain and then thought better of it. She didn't owe the cowboy any explanations.

He gave her jeans and blouse a disparaging glance. "You can wear those fancy duds of yours, but you'll be a lot more comfortable in these." He nodded at the worn jeans and shirt.

She knew when to admit defeat. "Where do I change?"

He made a production of looking about. "Our deluxe dressing rooms are that way." He gestured to a stand of scrawny trees.

Clothes in hand, she stalked toward the trees, fuming. How dare he? She was Star Whitney with a dozen blockbusters to her credit. Just as her temper reached the simmering stage, her sense of humor kicked in.

She breathed out a quiet laugh at herself. Obviously, the cowboy hadn't recognized her name. He probably didn't even go to the movies.

She had little patience with stars who demanded instant recognition. And hadn't she wished for some anonymity when she traveled? Looks like she got what she wanted.

She knew he thought her a snob when she'd refused to wear his clothes. He couldn't be further from the truth.

She pulled off her jeans and blouse and carefully folded them. Twenty-plus years of poverty weren't erased by a few years of success. No, she had learned her lessons well. Don't waste. Don't count on tomorrow. Above all, don't count on someone else to take care of you.

When she'd left her grandmother's house—it could never be called a home—and started on her own, she'd scrimped and saved to pay for acting lessons. That meant eating a lot of macaroni and shopping at thrift stores for her clothes.

After her first part, she'd splurged and bought her first new dress in five years, and vowed she'd never again wear other people's clothes. Granted, present circumstances were extreme, but she still found it hard to break her resolve.

She yanked on the shirt and then the jeans. He'd been right. The clothes weren't a bad fit at all.

Something slithered at her feet. She dropped the clothes she was holding and screamed for all she was worth.

Her yelp had Rafe coming at a run. "What the heck—"

"That." She pointed to the snake in a lethal coil not six inches from her feet.

He grabbed a stick, lifted the snake up, and tossed it aside.

She looked away when he crushed a rock against the snake's head.

"Rattlesnake. Looks like we've got tonight's dinner." The glint in his eyes was one step short of outright laughter.

She'd seen rattlesnake listed on the menus of tony restaurants. Snake, buffalo, and bear had all become gourmet fare. Her tastes ran to the pedestrian. Give her a greasy hamburger with fried onions any day.

She shuddered. Before she knew how it had happened, she was in his arms.

"It's all right," he murmured.

Too frightened to be embarrassed, she clung to him. He was strong and warm and very male. His denim shirt felt rough against her skin.

"I . . . uh . . . thank you." She prayed her cheeks weren't as red as they felt.

Her pulse still hadn't returned to normal. She knew it had as much to do with the lingering memory of being in his arms as it did with her recent scare.

"Yell if you see any more snakes." He picked up the snake and started back toward camp.

She had seen men equally as attractive before but never such a compelling one, and never had one made such an impact on her as had this one.

She made a face at his retreating back. He walked with a fascinating combination of arrogance and grace. It wasn't quite a strut, she thought with grudging honesty, but it came close.

Hollywood boasted some of the best-looking men on the planet, but none came close to Rafe Mackenzie.

Suddenly, she laughed as the absurdity of the situation struck her. She was stuck in the middle of nowhere with nothing but a cowboy with an attitude and a bunch of cows for company.

As with all the curves life had chosen to throw her way, she was determined to make the best of it.

Chapter Two

Sunset in the desert was nature at its best. The sun was riding low in the sky, all bleeding colors and fiery light. Heat still clung to the day, but she felt a bit of the evening cool.

Mere words were inadequate to describe the beauty before her. The quiet was unbroken save for the gentle lowing of the cattle and sounds of the camp. Even those were soothing.

She was besieged by color, the richness and the thickness of it. How had she ever thought the land dull, lifeless? It fairly vibrated with color—mauve and rose, violet and turquoise. She blinked, needing to rest her eyes for a moment from the brilliance that assailed her.

She liked looking at the cattle, without knowing why. She liked the sounds they made when the sun slipped below the horizon and the men talked quietly of long ago times. She even liked the smell of them, the rich, earthy smell that somehow didn't seem to stink even when she knew it should.

The camp was a hive of activity. Everyone had a job and set about doing it with quiet efficiency. Star felt as helpless as she knew she must look. Give her a saucepan and a stove and she could whip up a meal in minutes. A cast iron frying pan and an open flame were out of her experience.

Regardless of what Rafe thought, she was no snob. She'd worked her butt off for her grandmother, who believed in curbing a rebellious spirit with a scrub brush and lye soap. Star had spent more hours on her hands and knees with a bucket of soapy water than she cared to remember.

She caught several of the men giving her curious glances. She didn't mind. She was accustomed to men's stares. There was nothing to make her uncomfortable in the looks they cast her.

Star was beginning to put names to faces. Casey, the foreman, a stubby man with stubby hands. Johnny, barely out of his teens and whose eyes followed her everywhere she went, peppered her with questions. Dakota and Nevada, twins so much alike that she could tell them apart only by the faint scar above Nevada's left eye.

Johnny shuffled from foot to foot. "Star, I mean Ms. Whitney—"

"Star is fine."

"You are the prettiest thing I ever did see. Other than my girl, of course." The blush that worked its way up his face made him look younger than ever. He looked barely old enough to shave.

"You're pretty sharp-looking yourself."

His color deepened. "Would you . . . I mean could you . . . look at this letter I'm writing to her?" He shoved a much-folded piece of paper into her hands. "I figure a woman your age could give me some hints."

She'd been well and truly put in her place, Star reflected. She was officially an older woman.

She looked over the letter and hid a smile. "Maybe you should spend more time telling her how much you miss her rather than telling her about the cows."

He nodded eagerly. "Thank you, ma'am."

Now she was a *ma'am*. The idea tickled her sense of humor.

She watched in fascination as Casey cut and skewered the snake. He was small, grizzled, and wiry, but with a presence that more than made up for his lack of height.

The meat sizzled over the flame. She did her best to avoid looking at it, recalling how they'd happen to come by that particular snake. Her belly roiled in protest at the memory.

She finished the cornmeal muffin and canned fruit in record time. Unashamedly, she licked the fruit syrup from her fingers.

Rafe must have noticed for he gestured to the snake.

"You don't expect me to eat that." In truth, she was starving. She hadn't eaten since early morning. The continental breakfast at the hotel's dining room seemed days ago.

"Your choice." He stabbed a piece of meat with a fork. "Tastes like chicken."

Her traitorous stomach chose that moment to growl. Casey forked a piece of snake on to a plate and held it out to her.

After a moment's hesitation, she accepted it ginger-ly and bit into the meat. "It's good." She couldn't keep the surprise from her voice. Or the embarrassment. "Thanks."

" 'Course it's good," Casey said. "Rattler makes good eats." The lines around his mouth eased a bit.

She liked the foreman. His plain speaking and frankly ugly face topped with sparse ginger-colored hair were comforting. His boss was another matter. From the top of his Stetson to the tips of his battered boots, Rafe was every inch the cowboy. Curiosity stirred, and simple feminine pique. She'd charmed kings, presidents, and studio executives.

One smart-mouthed cowboy wasn't going to make her feel inferior because she hadn't grown up building fires and eating rattlesnake.

For the time being, they were stuck with each other. She'd make the best of it because she had no choice.

It was hard to complain, though, when the air turned cool and the light softened as the sun slumped lower in the west. She imagined the colors she'd admired a short time ago would mute to gray when the sun dropped below the peaks of the Rockies.

She stayed at the fire for a while longer, content to watch and listen. Light leaked out of the day, and the dusk edged toward night.

How long had it been since she'd watched the stars appear from their daytime hiding places? She'd nearly forgotten the beauty to be found in a sky of black velvet spangled with nature's own lighting.

Rafe settled back, prepared to enjoy himself as Casey launched into an improbable story. He watched Star. She propped her elbows on her knees, obviously hanging on to Casey's every word. Her face glowed with heightened color.

Rafe felt a shifting inside of him. It was Star, and the way she looked by the soft light of the campfire. He caught a glimpse of her mouth. It was soft and full and utterly feminine.

Did she have to turn so that her profile drew his attention to the graceful line of her neck? He studied the fine line of her jaw and the shell-shaped perfection of her ear.

He reminded himself he'd been burned before by a beautiful woman and had no wish to repeat the experience, but he wasn't getting the message. He caught Casey's sharp gaze. His old friend could read him as no one else could. A frown drew Casey's brows together in his rumpled face.

Rafe gave a short nod, as much in response to his

own resolve as to Casey's unspoken rebuke. He wasn't about to make a fool of himself over a woman. Particularly this woman. Spoiled and pampered, she probably never gave a thought to anyone but herself.

Still, he couldn't help but remember the patient way she'd answered Johnny's questions and the warmth of her smile when he introduced her to each of the men.

She looked as out of place at the campfire as a rose would among the ubiquitous sagebrush that tumbled across the prairie.

He noticed she drew closer to the fire. Without giving himself time to think about it, he went to her and dropped his jacket over her shoulders. "Easy does it," he said when she jumped.

She looked up at him, gaze locking with his. "Thanks." Something passed between them. She looked away, needing to break the spell.

"It gets cold here come dark." He paused. "We'll get you back where you belong. But it'll take a while."

The sound of his voice brushed her skin like the desert breeze, charged with electricity and sand. "Then I guess we're stuck with each other."

"Guess so."

Star spread out the sleeping roll Rafe had given her and prepared to slip inside it.

Someone was gently shaking her the following morning. Star usually awoke slowly, in stages, each successive cup of coffee bringing her into full consciousness.

"We leave in thirty minutes." Rafe stood over her.

"You could have woken me."

"I just did."

She was treated to a look at his morning face. The stubble that prickled his jaw had darkened, stressing the lines bracketing his mouth. Sleep-mussed hair fell across his forehead.

She scrambled up. "You have the manners of one of those cows you're so fond of," she said tartly.

"Steers."

She looked at him blankly.

"Those cows are steers, 'cept for a few mamas and their babies."

She gave him an impatient look. "Cows, steers. What's the difference? The point is—"

A slow grin stretched across his face. "To a bull, it makes a difference. A big difference."

A flush crept up her face to settle high on her cheeks. She walked with as much dignity as possible to the small clump of trees she'd used last night for a dressing room.

When she returned, she found Johnny waiting for her with a plate of food. He had the fresh-faced good looks of the very young. The sweet smile he gave her was balm to her spirit.

She wouldn't be human—or female—if she didn't respond to the boy's obvious admiration. He looked at her with such honest pleasure that she couldn't help but smile in return. His lips twitched in a shy but delighted grin.

His awe of her was even more touching when she remembered that he regarded her as a *ma'am*.

Over breakfast, Johnny filled her in on the other men, charming her with stories about Rafe and Casey and the rest. "Casey, he's crusty on the outside, but inside, he's soft as butter. Especially when it comes to Rafe and the ranch."

She kept that in mind.

Rafe found a sweet little mare for her. Wendy responded to the slightest touch of the heels with a disposition to match. The riding lessons Star had taken early in her career were paying off.

"You're a beauty," Star said as she patted the mare's neck. "A real beauty."

To her surprise, she discovered she was enjoying the work. It required a certain amount of muscle, but little thought. She was tired of thinking, of trying to balance the demands of her work, the business decisions, the arguments with her agent. It was a relief to simply do her job and let her mind drift.

Though not of her choosing, her situation suited her very well. There was nothing urgent calling her back at the moment. She could take this time for herself. Hadn't that been what she'd intended all along? She was just taking a different mode of transportation.

The last two days had shifted her priorities. Life on the trail had gotten her out of her head and into her body and emotions. Without the pressures of work, she was seeing clearer than she had in months, maybe years.

After some reflection, she had decided to keep her identity to herself. None of the men had recognized her, and it would only give fuel to Rafe's claims that she was a spoiled city woman if she let on that she was an actress.

By noon, Star was feeling the effects of riding. Her hips and legs ached as they hadn't since the time she'd been thrown by a horse and dragged a few feet while she was on location.

She blinked, trying to see beyond the midday glare. The sun leached the ground of all color. A hot breeze whispered over her skin. Sweat gathered at the nape of her neck. She swiped at it with the kerchief Rafe had loaned her.

Traditional red and black, it was worn around the edges, thin in places. She felt much the same. Worn around the edges and thin in places. Surviving in Hollywood had done that to her. That and knowing she was drifting in her career, in her personal life.

She couldn't help the comparison between the open prairie and the city. She loved her adopted home, the energy and intensity of it. But she wasn't immune to its drawbacks—the noise and lights that never shut down, the brittle talk and minced walk. Billboards flashing in neon colors, the film of smog that coated everything from the grass to the glass skyscrapers. The dirt that clung to the city even on a rainy day.

It was the city. She loved it, even as she recognized its flaws.

The rhythm of the horses' hooves on the sun-hardened ground lulled her into a state of drowsy contentment. The hat Rafe had provided her cast just enough shade to protect her eyes. She slumped before jerking herself upright.

"Careful," Rafe said and reached out a steadying hand. "You don't want to end up as roadkill."

The offhand way he said it made her hackles rise. "Thanks for the concern."

"Any time." He rode off, leaving her to stare after him. In his eyes, she could do nothing right, including setting a horse. Of course, she hadn't given him much reason to think otherwise.

In reflex, her hands tightened on the reins, and the mare tossed her head in protest. Star relaxed her grip, chagrined to find she'd taken out her frustrations on the animal.

"It's all right," she murmured.

Wendy responded to the soothing noises and settled down.

Star squared her shoulders. She'd show Rafe that she had starch in her backbone. She'd change his mind. Or die trying. The dramatic, if silent vow, caused her to chuckle at herself. At least, she still had her sense of humor.

She'd prove he was wrong about her, and prove something to herself as well.

When they stopped that evening, there was a flurry of activity. "What's up?" she asked Johnny.

"One of the cows is dropping a calf."

Star flinched in sympathy with each groan the cow gave, and winced at the contractions. After an hour, the poor animal looked exhausted. Too tired to even lift her head, she looked up at the humans with a pleading expression in her brown eyes.

Casey scowled. "She ain't moving it the way she should."

Rafe knelt to check. "I've got to turn it." He washed his hands and arms in a bucket of water.

Star watched in fascination as he reached inside the animal. "What's he doing?"

"He's pulling the calf through . . . the birth canal," Johnny said, a flush staining his young face.

Within a few minutes, a hoof appeared. Rafe pulled until he caught a leg. When the calf came out, with a spurt of blood and fluid, Star felt tears dampen her cheeks.

She wasn't put off by the mess. On the contrary, she had enjoyed witnessing the small drama.

"A summer calf," Johnny said, wiping down the calf. "Ain't he pretty? Summer calves are always slick ones."

She thought about it. Slick was the right word, she decided, for the small animal who was already nuzzling his mother. She knelt beside him, reaching out a hand to pet his quivering sides. "Aren't you the prettiest thing," she crooned.

The calf ignored her and stood on shaking legs, his concentration fixed upon finding his mother.

Star looked on, transfixed by the sight of mother and baby.

Rafe watched, something twisting in his heart at the picture she made. She didn't appear to care that she was smearing her clothes with blood and birth fluids as she petted the calf, and he felt a glimmer of admiration. Her hands were coated with both, grimy with dirt. She seemed oblivious to it, intent on her task. Her expression was tender, almost soft. A damp gaze muted the brightness of her eyes. Tears?

Her look was one of delight. He felt a quick surge of pleasure himself. It didn't mean anything, he reminded himself.

He caught a whiff of her scent. Even on the trail, she managed to smell soap-and-water fresh. It was as heady as the most exotic perfume. He experienced the same flare of reluctant attraction he had the first time he'd laid eyes on her. He wondered if she, too, felt the electricity between them, not unlike the spark in the air before a lightning strike.

She was deliberately trying to drive him insane. Everything about her seemed designed to turn him inside out.

He hooked his thumbs in his pockets. He didn't understand his dissatisfaction. The tension had been growing between them, building and shifting like a summer storm.

"What's the matter, princess? Haven't you ever seen

a calving before?" Irritation with her, with himself, rimmed his voice.

Stupid question. Of course she hadn't seen a calving. Not many city folk had. He was about to apologize when her lips trembled.

"No." Shadows gathered in her eyes, dulling their earlier brightness. There was such vulnerability in her face that he reached out a hand, wanting to comfort, realizing he didn't know how.

He felt like the kind of creep who went around kicking dogs and terrorizing small children. "Look, I'm sorry—"

"Forget it."

"I didn't mean—" He raked a hand through his hair. Her eyes were wide and tear-shiny. "I can be a real jerk sometimes."

"Yeah. You can." She took off.

He never claimed to have any smooth lines. He didn't have the time or the inclination to spout pretty words and was plain spoken to the point of bluntness. His ex-fiancee had told him that he had all the sophistication of a backwards mule.

Still, he didn't usually alienate women—anyone—so quickly. Then again, the sight of a woman didn't usually slam into him like a bare-knuckled fist. Considering that, he thought he might be cut some slack for not being at his best.

More than that, though, it wasn't like him to make judgments of someone he didn't know. Integrity warred with long, ingrained prejudice. When he'd gotten the frustration out of his system, he started in the direction Star had taken. He prided himself upon being a fair man. He owed her an apology.

"I'm sorry," he said when he caught up with her. "I was out of line back there."

She looked adorable in the too-big jeans and shirt, face bare of makeup, hair pulled back in a ponytail. It didn't make the words of apology come any easier.

"It's all right." Her voice was stiff with hurt.

He'd done that. He knew it, was powerless to undo it. He watched her move away, telling himself to let her go this time. Leave bad enough alone.

He resented the protective instincts she roused within him almost as much as he did his attraction to her. He didn't know what happened whenever he was with the pretty lady. She was as slim as a wand, but she packed a powerful presence, managing to destroy whatever claim he had on good sense.

He dug a finger in the center of his brow, trying to relieve the tension that had gathered there. He didn't have to watch to know that Star had managed to charm the other men. That she did it effortlessly caused his already frayed temper to worsen. Dog in the manger, he thought with disgust. That it was directed at himself didn't lessen his annoyance.

Hadn't he already decided that a woman in the camp was trouble, especially one like Star, who relied on her looks to get what she wanted?

The unfairness of that rankled. As far as he knew, she hadn't asked for any special favors. Fact was, she was conscientious to a fault in doing the chores assigned her.

It was getting harder and harder to ignore her effect on him.

That sharpened his voice. "We don't have time to stand around mooning over a scrawny calf," he said to the men, his friends, who had watched what went down with frank interest. "Get back to work."

The men exchanged looks he couldn't miss. So he wasn't going to win any popularity contests. He had more important things on his mind.

When everyone, including Star, gave him a wide berth for the remainder of the evening, he knew he'd better mend fences.

His men looked almost as embarrassed at hearing him stumble through an apology as he felt in making it. One of them made a bad joke, and the matter was forgotten.

Who was he angry at? Himself, he guessed.

He rubbed the kinks from his neck. It didn't help.

Star reached up a hand to smooth back her hair. He recognized the reaction as a nervous one. He traced the movement of her hand, and remembered the softness of it on his skin earlier.

Proximity, he reasoned, would account for the attraction he experienced. She was a beautiful woman.

A calf bawled, disturbing the stillness of the night. A

few moments later a cow answered. The familiar sounds soothed him.

Casey usually knew when to keep his mouth shut and his thoughts to himself. It was one of the things that made him so valuable. So when he decided to put in his two cents worth about Star, Rafe was more than annoyed.

Casey shot a look in Star's direction. "Pretty lady."

"Yeah."

"A woman like that could tangle a man up." He waited a beat. "If he let her."

"Don't worry. I learned my lesson with Gina."

It had taken time, but Rafe had gotten over the anger when Gina, his fiancee, had walked out on him. What he hadn't totally rid himself of was the guilt and the betrayal. Sometimes he doubted he'd ever be free of the memories that still had the power to shred his heart.

Casey cleared his throat. "Just don't let her keep you from doing what you have to. You know what depends on this roundup."

Rafe gave a short nod. "I know." Too well, he knew.

Chapter Three

It had been four days. Four long days. Her body said it had been even longer. She was sore, stiff, and filthy. She'd gladly give the earnings from her last movie for a shower. The sponge bath she'd made do with last night left a lot to be desired.

The day started early, before daybreak. An hour later, they were mounted and on their way.

Star concentrated on staying seated, but she couldn't help glancing in Rafe's direction. He sat a horse as easily as studio producers rode their executive chairs behind glossy desks. She took a moment to admire the way worn denim snugged over muscular legs.

Aware that he was subjecting her to the same scrutiny she had dispensed, she met his gaze and let him take his time. After long moments, he gave a curt nod and tapped his heels against the big gelding.

An hour later, she shifted in the saddle, trying to find a more comfortable position. After spending several minutes at it without success, she gave it up and tried to concentrate on something else.

She glanced around, as much to take her mind off her discomfort as to satisfy her curiosity. The scenery, however, was stark enough to hold her attention. The dry gully bordering the trail was mute evidence of the drought that savaged the land. Rocks whitened by the sun glinted in the near blinding light.

A hard land. Like the trail boss. Her delight in yesterday's birthing had quickly evaporated. Rafe's sarcasm had seen to that.

She'd learned, the hard way, that a soft heart wasn't an asset in her chosen profession. Showing her emotions—off-screen—was tantamount to admitting weakness. Sure, tantrums and rudeness were the stuff of celebrity gossip columns. She knew actors and actresses who used both to advantage. But feelings, real feelings, were off limits.

It had become ingrained to keep her feelings to herself, as well as her work with abused children at a special home. Too much of a star's life was public fodder. What she did with the kids was private. It was for her, not for the publicity it might garner. Not for praise from her colleagues. Even her agent didn't know.

She knew most men saw her as purposely remote. That had always been fine with her. Her agent said it added a nice touch of mystery to the persona of Star Whitney. Much better, she thought, than anyone knowing the truth, that, outside of her acting, she was terribly shy.

She'd learned to shield herself with a protective veneer, but somehow Rafe had managed to shatter it without breaking a sweat.

She didn't like being dependent upon him anymore than he wanted the responsibility for her. Away from everything and everyone she knew, she felt helpless, just as she had as a child. Then she'd had to depend upon her grandmother for everything, a woman who was as miserly with her affection as she was with her money.

Her grandmother had been fond of quoting scripture, pointing out those passages concerning pride, and predicting Star's doom.

Star had been too full of untidy wants, unruly thoughts, and ardent ambitions to accept her grandmother's pious preaching with equanimity.

She hadn't minded her grandmother's miserly ways as much as she had the verbal abuse the woman heaped upon her at every opportunity.

"You won't amount to anything. Just like your ma. She run off with that no-account foreigner with his fancy-shmancy ways. He left her with a babe in her belly and not a cent to her name. She came home like a whipped dog, tail between her legs, wanting me to take her in."

At this point, her scrawny bosom would heave in righteous memory. "I did my Christian duty. Took care of her when she gave birth to you two months early." A bony finger wagged in Star's face. It was this last which her grandmother took particular delight in. The litany occasionally varied, but the bitterness was always the same.

Star had learned to tune out the poisonous words, but the acid tone was harder to ignore. Her grandmother had used her charity as a stick to rout any spark of creativity or individuality she detected in Star.

She still bore the scars.

The "no-account foreigner," her father, had promised to come back for her mother, but he'd died in a car accident on his way back from Mexico.

When Star was born, her mother had named her Estrella. Her grandmother had fought against the name and insisted the child be called by the anglicized version, Star.

For the first . . . and last time, Star's mother had stood up to her overbearing mother, and Estrella it was. Until her mother's death. Never strong, her mother had succumbed to an infection that had moved to her heart. Star believed she'd died of a broken heart.

She had been five then. Estrella was no more.

Star had always felt like an embarrassment to her grandmother, her dark hair and gold skin proof of her mixed heritage. She'd once wondered if her grand-mother would love her if she apologized for being born.

When she brought home papers from school with GREAT WORK scrawled across the top, her grandmother had found something to criticize, something to remind Star that she was never good enough.

Her reaction had been hurt and bewilderment and a burning determination to succeed. She'd worked to make the honor roll, to win the class election, to be captain of her cheerleading team. Her grandmother's tepid praise was almost as hard to bear as was her biting criticism.

Star tried harder.

She had scrutinized herself, trying to discover what disgraced her in her grandmother's eyes. She looked for faults, and found them. She was too tall, too skinny. She wasn't smart enough or pretty enough or talented enough.

Finally, she'd accepted that nothing would win love where none existed.

Ironically, it was the looks her grandmother so hated that had garnered Star her first part. The Hispanic-Anglo combination of dark hair, blue eyes, and gold skin had caught a director's attention.

She owed her grandmother a debt. Hadn't that anger, that sense of never being good enough, when she'd walked out of that oppressive house, pushed her to where she was today?

Would she have scraped and clawed her way to the

top of her profession if she'd found any love at the place that had never been a home?

No, she admitted. She would have fantasized over becoming an actress, but she feared she wouldn't have done it. She wouldn't have found the courage. It had taken her grandmother's constant belittling for Star to risk going down that path.

Rafe pulled up at her side. "Come with me while I look for strays."

She nodded, determined she'd give him nothing to find fault with her. Once more, she noted easy grace with which he rode.

The way her thoughts kept straying to him brought her up short.

When had she started thinking about him in those terms? Then again, a lot of her behavior had been out of the ordinary since she had met him. The man posed a real threat to the carefully erected defenses that had protected her for years.

There was power in his gaze and a sense of pride of ownership as he looked out over the herd of cattle. He treated the land with a kind of reverence that went far beyond the politically correct environmentalism her Hollywood friends spouted.

She examined his face in the strong light of the sun. Unapologetically angled, it was not particularly handsome. His features were too strong, too compelling for the pretty-boy good looks like those of Hollywood's leading men.

No, his face would never be termed handsome. But it was attractive in a way that invited the viewer to take a second . . . and a third look. It hinted at the strength that was so much a part of him.

It was his eyes, though, that captivated her, eyes that saw everything and mirrored little of his own thoughts.

At the moment, they settled on her with such intensity that she had to resist the desire to squirm. With an effort, she steadied her breathing.

Rafe called a halt for lunch. She welcomed the break from the constant jarring of the ride.

He dismounted, then came around to her side and helped her down, his hands warm on her waist. She felt her heart gave a nervous jerk at his nearness.

She reminded herself that she was too smart to fall for a ruggedly handsome face. So she found him attractive. She'd known lots of attractive men.

The feelings she had for Rafe might have taken her unaware, but now that she recognized them for what they were, she could put them in perspective. She was grateful to him for rescuing her. That was all. Her breath came easier now.

After they finished their lunch, he policed the area, picking up a discarded tissue and handing it to her. "Take nothing but memories, leave nothing but footprints."

Ashamed, she stared at it. "I'm sorry. I wasn't thinking." That wasn't strictly true. She had been thinking. Just not about the consequences of littering. She'd been thinking about him, and only him.

Her earlier resolve slipped. She was falling for him, she thought a trifle desperately. For a smart woman, she'd been incredibly stupid. Still, she wasn't going to apologize for her feelings. Nor was she going to act on them.

The screech of a prairie falcon had her looking up. The sight of the bird gliding through the cloud-dusted sky transfixed her. Nothing in her life had prepared her for the untouched beauty she witnessed. She watched as it swooped to pounce upon a rabbit, then soar upward once more, the prey in its talons.

"It's beautiful," she said, the spread of her arms encompassing the land and sky and the slice of life they'd just witnessed.

"Most city folk get put off at the idea of wild animals hunting their food."

"Maybe I'm not most city folk."

He gave her one of those enigmatic looks that left her wondering what he was thinking. He curled a knuckle under her chin and tilted her face to his. "You'll do."

The thank you she'd been about to say died before she could give voice to it. *You'll do*. What had he meant by that? The feelings she'd entertained abruptly vanished. How did he propel her from tenderness to exasperation so quickly?

The man was clearly impossible. She opened her mouth to tell him just that when he smiled, a lazy slide of amusement.

His smile changed everything about him in a way she hadn't expected, threatening to take her breath away. It ought to be declared a lethal weapon, she thought, not altogether charitably.

A high-pitched bawl diverted her attention. She scrambled to the edge of a cliff. A calf was stranded halfway down.

"Rafe. Over here."

Within seconds, he was at her side.

"I'm going down." He looped a rope around his waist, and tied it to his saddle horn.

With the horse anchoring him, he climbed down. Going up, with a forty-pound calf under his arm, was another matter.

Star pulled and prayed in equal measure while Bear slowly backed up.

He wasn't going to make it.

"Hold on," she called. "I'm coming down."

He shook his head.

She paid no attention. She followed his example and climbed down a rope tied to Wendy's saddle horn.

Sharing the calf's weight, they made the tricky climb to the top of the cliff. Concerned for the calf and for Rafe, she grew careless and faltered.

To catch herself, she braced her right leg against the face of the rock. Her hands slipped on the rope, and she banged her ankle against the face of the rock. Pain shot up her leg. She ignored it and focused on reaching the top, her breath coming in sharp puffs.

Rafe set the calf down, brushed himself off, and replaced his hat. It was all done with such calm that she lost whatever control she'd achieved in those interminable moments when he was suspended over the cliff.

"Don't you ever do that again," she said, fear and anger trembling in her voice.

"I'd do the same for you."

"That's different."

Rafe's lips kicked up. "Why? I've known that calf a lot longer than I've known you."

It surprised her that he could make her laugh.

The fear that had lodged in her throat came rushing back. "You could've gotten yourself killed." That was the real source of her anger. Understanding it didn't make her feel any better.

"I didn't know you cared."

"I don't." Not for the world would she tell him that her heart had stopped beating for the minutes he'd hung over the cliff. She rubbed a hand over her chest to make sure it was still thumping. "I don't. But I can't get out of here by myself."

"Princess," he drawled, "you're going to give me the wrong impression if you keep up that kind of sweet-talking."

She narrowed her eyes. "Listen, cowboy—"

"You weren't bad back there."

Her mouth dropped open in astonishment at the casually given compliment.

He checked the calf out, large hands gentle as they moved over limbs and joints, eyes intent on his task.

For a moment she wondered what it would feel like to have him kiss her with the same tenderness. She squashed the thought before it had fully formed. Mackenzie was a cowboy with an attitude. He made it clear what he thought of her each time he called her by that ridiculous name.

She wondered if he had read her mind for he stood and ran a casual finger down her arm. She bit back a gasp and barely managed not to jerk away. Wouldn't he like that?

She'd never known such a powerful affinity for a man in such a short time. Never known such a powerful affinity, period. She'd be a fool to act on it. In a few days, a week at most, they'd part ways.

He wrapped an arm around her waist, bringing her flush to him. "Thanks for what you did. That took guts."

It was the same voice he used when talking to his horse, with a gentle edge that managed to both soothe and praise. Despite her better judgment, she felt herself responding to it, and her pulse tripped a little faster.

She reminded herself that he didn't particularly like her, that they would go their separate ways in a few days, and yet here she was lapping up a few kind words like a hungry kitten with a bowl full of milk.

"You're welcome." The voice didn't sound like hers. In fact, nothing she did lately was like her.

Like now. When she wanted to know more about him

and dared to ask. Her gaze settled on his turquoise medallion. Set in silver, it was nearly as big as her first. "That's a beautiful medallion."

He fingered the silver filigree work that surrounded it. "My pa gave it to me when I turned twelve. His pa gave it to him when he was the same age. Said it was to remind me of where I'd come from and where I wanted to go."

She could picture him at twelve years old, hair the color of wet sand, a cowlick and freckles, his slow smile working its way up to his eyes.

It was an appealing picture, but no more so than the one he made now with his finger-combed hair and tanned, rugged face. It was a face etched with the lines of hard work. Sun and wind had carved ridges around his mouth, between his brows. They only added to his attraction.

"It's beautiful," she said once more.

"Beautiful," he agreed, but his eyes were on her. He touched one blunt fingertip to her chin, urging her to meet his gaze.

The world shifted into sharp focus as she suddenly became acutely aware of her surroundings—the smell of dust, the screech of a distant hawk, the stray strand of her own hair as it clung to her cheek.

She swallowed past the hitch in her throat. Rafe Mackenzie ought to be declared a natural hazard. He was too good looking for a woman's peace of mind. If only it was just infatuation she felt for him, but it was more. He put her in mind of an old-fashioned western hero with old-fashioned values, like honor, courage, and integrity.

"You remind me of my fiancee," he said unexpectedly.

She watched shadows slide into his eyes. "Fiancee?"

"Gina. She was almost as beautiful as you." The shadows deepened. "I met her on a trip to the city. We fell in love, thought we could make it work. She came for a visit. She lasted three months. Said she couldn't take the isolation, the winters."

"What happened?" she asked, sensing there was more to the story.

"She left with my best friend. Took off on a January day. Their car skidded, went over a mountain road."

She longed to soothe away the anguish she read in his eyes but knew better than to offer comfort where none was wanted. She understood he blamed himself. Because she couldn't do anything to change what had happened, she listened.

"She's dead because she was trying to get away from me." He laughed, a sound not of humor but of bitterness and guilt.

She didn't know what to say. The sound of pain in his voice was fresh and raw, from a wound that had never healed. She hurt for him, for herself, for a woman she'd never met.

He closed his eyes briefly. When they opened, there was the memory of misery in them.

Star felt some unbreachable barrier form between

them—the shadow of Gina, the fiancee who'd walked away from him and then died. She wanted, more than she'd ever wanted anything, to erase the hollow look in his eyes and replace it with warmth.

She watched as he struggled with the millstone of guilt, shoulders braced against it. He turned on his heel, primed to walk away from the past, away from her.

She put a hand on his arm. "Rafe?"

He paused, turned to face her. A flicker of irritation ran over his face.

"Don't walk away from me. You just shared a part of yourself with me."

His lips twisted in a parody of a smile. "It's ancient history. It doesn't matter anymore."

"Doesn't it?" Her hands weren't quite steady as she flattened them against his chest. "You couldn't stop what happened. You can only control what you do. The same way I can only control what I do."

She felt the pounding of hooves before she actually heard it. Seconds passed before the meaning of the sound registered.

Casey arrived. "You two okay?"

Rafe's answer was short in the extreme. "Fine."

Breathing space. The arrival of the others had given them both breathing space, and she was determined to take advantage of it.

"You were gone so long we got worried. Guess there weren't no need." The drawl in Casey's voice was thick enough to cut with a knife.

"No need," Rafe agreed and rested his hand at her waist. "We rescued this little fellow," he said, drawing the attention to the calf.

Casey nodded shortly. "Good. His ma's been bawling for him."

She chanced a look at Rafe, and noted the remote look in his eyes. The shared moment of intimacy was over. They were back to the parts he had assigned them. She'd played countless roles over the years. She'd play this one. What's more, she'd survive.

She was centered once more, her thoughts focused on when she would get back to her life, her work. That was all that mattered.

Rafe swung the calf over his saddle and climbed up behind. She made sure to keep a distance between herself and Rafe for the rest of the day. She couldn't afford the disturbing feelings she experienced whenever he was near. She didn't—couldn't—meet his eyes, but she knew he was watching her, every fiber of him as aware of her as she was of him.

His revelation about his failed engagement had startled her, and surprised her that she cared. It was none of her concern. Most of the men she met in the industry had a broken relationship or two behind them. Perhaps that was why she had never even become engaged. Marriage was too serious a commitment to be taken lightly. She'd seen too many marriages crumble. When she gave her heart, it would be forever.

When they stopped for the day, she was pathetically

grateful to rest. She moved with deliberate slowness, her legs wobbly from the constant riding.

But it was her ankle that bothered her the most. She could scarcely put her weight on it.

She hoped Rafe hadn't noticed that she was limping. She didn't want him being kind to her. Right now, she didn't need *kind*. She needed someone snapping at her, making her angry. Making her cope.

She looked up, caught him watching her. It looked like her prayers had been answered. The look in his eyes was definitely not *kind*.

The sounds of the night receded, and all she heard was her own breathing.

It had been four days. Four days in which Rafe worked to convince himself that he wasn't interested in his uninvited guest.

He needed time, distance.

Lots of time.

Lots of distance.

His reaction to Star made a mockery of his attempt to ignore her effect on him. He didn't want to be anywhere near this woman who was fast getting under his skin. Yet here he was, sitting not two feet from her, her scent wrapping its way around him, holding him hostage with invisible strings.

He hadn't slept in four days. He was as cranky as a just-birthed calf bawling for its mother.

Though the day was melting into twilight, heat still

bounced off the land. He wanted to blame her for that too. What was worse, he hadn't done anything without thinking of her. Inexorably, his gaze strayed to her.

Although he'd take being staked out in the desert by a red ant hill and covered with honey before admitting it, he'd enjoyed her company. She had a quick sense of humor and a sharp mind, not to mention that looking at her was pure pleasure.

That was precisely why he chose a spot on the other side of the campfire from her come dinner time.

Casey had fixed the meal; skillet biscuits and canned stew. Rafe noticed with wicked amusement that Star had no trouble putting down her share of the food tonight. Apparently, her sophisticated tastes had taken a turn for the worse, or the better, he thought with a grin he was careful to keep to himself.

He caught Casey's broad wink. Apparently Rafe wasn't the only one having an inward chuckle over Star.

She hadn't said much during supper. He suspected she didn't have the energy to do more than pull off her boots and curl up in her sleeping bag. She'd worked hard, surprising him into grudging admiration.

She did her part in cleaning up. Were her movements a bit stiff? He didn't have a chance to ask her about it before Casey started in on a story.

Rafe listened with half an ear, his attention still drawn by Star. Even after a full day of sitting a horse and eating dust, she was lovely. Her hair was twisted on top of her head, held by a couple of pins, and all he could think about was letting it down.

Her face was bare of makeup, and her cheek bore a smudge of dirt. Silhouetted by the campfire, she looked quietly serene. Yet he'd witnessed firsthand the spark that simmered beneath those lovely eyes. Those same eyes made him weak. Not much did that to him anymore.

She cocked her head, and an enchanting little dimple appeared at the corner of her mouth. One more thing to notice about her.

The lady was a paradox, classy right down to her manicured fingertips but feisty as all get-out when riled. She reminded him of one of the Arabians his father used to breed. Fine-boned with a proud bearing. All temperament and nervous energy one moment and sweetly docile the next.

The dichotomy intrigued him and warned him away in the same moment. It didn't help that his gaze followed her wherever she went.

He was starting to like her. The knowledge shook the carefully placed barriers he had erected around his heart.

More than once, she'd managed to surprise him, but he couldn't be certain she wasn't as grasping and selfish as Gina had been. If he'd learned anything from his ex-fiancee, it was not to give his trust . . . or his heart . . . so easily. A beautiful face didn't always reflect the soul within.

Maybe he'd expected too much of Gina. A beautiful woman, she'd wanted, needed, the admiration of all men. He'd seen signs of it before asking her to marry him but had convinced himself that their love was strong enough to overcome any problems.

He'd been wrong.

The other men laughed appreciatively as Casey finished the story. "Tell us another one," Johnny urged.

Rafe knew them all and never tired of hearing the tall tales. Tonight, though, his thoughts kept straying to Star. He wished the rapt expression on her face was directed at him rather than Casey.

The cattle stirred, the rumbling noise as distinctive to a rancher as the sound of his own breathing. He was content to let his thoughts drift.

Star had let her hair down, her movements echoing his imagination of moments ago. She began brushing the glorious length of it, and he realized that he'd been waiting for just that. Each night the ritual had dug deeper inside him. Each night he asked himself why the sight of a woman brushing her hair had such an impact on him.

She murmured that she'd better turn in. She made a trip to the straggly stand of trees and returned within a few minutes.

Rafe frowned. Was she limping a bit? He was about to ask her when Casey waylaid him with a question about tomorrow's route.

By the time they'd hashed over the pros and cons of

various trails, Star had already spread out her sleeping bag and appeared to be asleep.

He stopped long enough to check on her, make sure she had settled in. After assuring himself she was all right, he lifted his gaze to the glimmering stars overhead. "Sleep well, princess."

Whether he wanted to or not, he knew he'd spend the night thinking of her.

Chapter Four

By the fifth day, Star could scarcely walk. She managed to get on her horse and hold on. The hours passed with agonizing slowness. She didn't try to do more than simply stay seated. Exhaustion dragged at her.

Her ankle had swollen overnight. Somehow, she'd managed to get her boot over it this morning. Pain pulsed through her in unrelenting waves.

A thousand times she'd wanted to call it quits, to tell Rafe she couldn't go another mile. A thousand times, she'd held her tongue. She wouldn't give him a reason to find fault with her.

She'd prove to him that she wasn't a quitter. She felt someone staring at her and turned to find him watching her, eyes narrowed.

Tell him that you can't go on.

The words trembled on the tip of her tongue, but she bit them back. She wouldn't give him the satisfaction of hearing her beg for a rest. That was exactly what he expected from her: Whining complaints.

Irritation gleamed briefly in his eyes. And something more. Something that looked suspiciously like admiration. She looked again and decided she'd been mistaken. The time they'd spent together yesterday, the sweet kiss, might never have happened.

Well, she wasn't out to win any popularity contests. Right now, all she wanted was to get out of this place with her skin intact. Once more, she shifted in her saddle.

Her only solace was that nobody had noticed she was barely holding it together. She was an even better actress than the reviews gave her credit for, she decided with grim humor.

She had played a role where the heroine had succumbed to a fever. In the film, the hero, a bounty hunter, had taken care of her, sacrificing catching the bad guy to stay with her.

It had been a romantic movie, with a hero women grew dreamy-eyed over and a story line designed to wring tears from the hardest of hearts.

So why was she thinking about that now? She was a little tired, stiff from the long hours in the saddle. That was all. No way was she going to complain and add fuel to Rafe's charge that she was nothing more than a spoiled city woman.

She gritted her teeth. She'd prove him wrong and prove something to herself along the way. Her upbringing had taught her that the only person she could depend on was herself.

She had no one to blame but herself. Pride goeth before a fall, her grandmother had frequently quoted to her. Star grimaced. She had pride to spare.

She'd worked too hard to allow a stubborn cowboy to strip away her self-confidence. With her ankle throbbing, she had difficulty finding purchase in the stirrup. The pain grew until she could barely keep upright. Sheer will kept her holding on to the reins.

Heat rippled over the prairie, causing her to pull the brim of her hat down to shade her eyes. She tipped her canteen back and drank deeply. The tepid water tasted like nectar, and she felt marginally better. She needed food and eight hours sleep. Come morning, she'd be fine. She didn't even bother trying to believe her own lie.

By the time Rafe called a halt, she couldn't move. Her hands remained on the reins, the only thing that kept her from toppling over.

"Your turn to help with the fire," Rafe said. He turned away to talk with Casey.

Right now she had more serious problems than a hard-headed cowboy. She gazed down at the ground, which appeared to be miles away.

She swung a leg over the saddle, intending to slide down. Weariness made her clumsy, causing her to land harder than she'd intended. Her right ankle gave way, and she fell.

Rafe moved quickly, but not quickly enough.

She crumpled to the ground, crying out as she did so.

He was at her side in seconds and lifted her in his arms. The word he muttered would have earned him a tongue-lashing from his ma . . . after she'd washed his mouth out with soap first.

He looked at her face, pale beneath its gold tones. She felt small and fragile in his hands.

The moan that escaped her lips was so quickly suppressed he might have imagined it if not for her involuntary flinch.

"Why didn't you say something?" He didn't wait for an answer. He remembered his first roundup. He'd been so tired he could scarcely put one foot in front of the other by the end of the day. He'd have passed out if his pa hadn't had the sense to call a halt and given Rafe a day to recover.

He cradled Star against his chest, loathe to let her go.

He barked out a couple of orders. Within minutes, the men had set up a shelter of blankets and brought him the supplies he needed.

He carried her to the makeshift tent and laid her down as gently as he could. "Stubborn woman." But the words were said without heat. Right now, he was concerned with getting her boot off without hurting her.

She was weak as a baby but still made a feeble

attempt to swat his hands away. He ignored that. She pulled at him. Not her weakness, but her strength, the strength he was only now beginning to appreciate. He had to respect that, just as he had to admit to the attraction that simmered between them.

He eased the boot down her leg. When the boot slid over her injured ankle, she gasped.

"Sorry." He didn't trust himself to say more.

"It's all right."

"What happened to it?"

"Banged it . . . against rock . . . other day."

And he understood. She'd hurt herself helping him pull up the calf. He wrapped the ankle the best he could.

Star didn't utter a word during the process.

It was her very silence that tore at his insides. How had he branded her spoiled? Tears and complaints he could have accepted, had expected. But determination and pride? Those were qualities he hadn't counted on. The spine of steel beneath the fragile shell was unbelievably appealing.

Her vulnerability called to mind all of his protective instincts, and at the same time, made him feel totally helpless.

He helped her up to take a couple of painkillers, cradling the back of her neck with his hand. The way she nestled against his side, resting her head in the curve of his shoulder, seemed the most natural thing in the world.

She turned on her side. "Rafe." He watched her lips curve as she said his name. "Thank you."

He didn't deserve her gratitude.

"Are you angry at me?" she asked drowsily.

"No . . ." His words came to a stop as he realized she was asleep.

A surge of tenderness coursed through him. Unable to help himself, he brushed a strand of hair back from her face. He contented himself to simply watch her.

He didn't have time for a woman, least of all a woman like Star, city-bred, who could have no place in his world. Hadn't he learned his lesson? If not, he was going to this time.

Hard upon that came the lowering thought that the lady was more than he'd first thought. He felt a rush of remorse that he'd misjudged her so completely.

It had undone him to see her in pain, torn him into little pieces. No way could he leave her with someone else. She was his responsibility, and his alone.

If she'd wanted to make him feel like a jerk, it had worked. In spades. What would his reaction have been if she'd asked him to slow down, to take it a bit easier? He was afraid he knew.

He had pushed her deliberately, in an attempt to prove that she couldn't handle trail life.

This woman had both spunk and courage. She had shown him both, and, at the same time, had shown him up.

*   *   *

When Casey showed up, Star tried a smile. The scowl he shot at her drained all warmth from his eyes. She'd made an enemy here and had no idea why.

Casey gestured in Rafe's direction.

"He's taken a shine to you. You keep him from what he needs to do. If he don't finish this roundup, he'll lose everything." His faded eyes took on a hard glint. "Likely as not, he will anyway. But he has a chance. Or he did." He cut the words short, as though he had said more than he'd intended. His leathery face, with the seams, wrinkles and grooves, scarcely moved, though his eyes spoke volumes.

She understood his animosity now. "Rafe didn't tell me. I'm sorry." The inadequacy of the word shamed her.

"Sorry doesn't help." He took off after that, leaving her to stew over his words. Guilt left a nasty taste in her mouth.

She made her own decisions. She had never been one to sit idly by and let others decide her fate.

When Rafe came to change her bandages, she struggled to sit up. "I can travel." The words stuck in her throat as the pain snaked through her. She looked at him in frustration. "You can't stay here."

"Why not?"

"Your cattle." Her voice was low as guilt ate at her. She knew what it was to claw, to scratch to make a living. If Rafe lost his cattle because of her, she would never forgive herself.

He muttered something about people who didn't know when to mind their own business.

"Don't you dare blame Casey. At least he had the courtesy of telling me the truth."

A muscle jumped in Rafe's cheek, but his voice remained smooth. "The truth is that what I say goes. Casey takes orders from me."

He fitted a finger beneath her chin, raising her head so that her gaze was on a level with his own. "You can't travel. I can't leave you here alone. End of story."

She saw the determination in his eyes. She wouldn't win this battle of wills. "Have it your way."

"I usually do." A slow smile, both rueful and teasing, curled the corners of his lips.

He made light of it. Yet she knew what it must have cost him to stay behind, to leave what was his in the hands of others. Rafe was a throwback to another century when men fought to keep what was theirs. Now he was stuck here, because of her.

Here was a man who did what needed to be done, and did what was right without thinking about it, and who did it without puffing himself up with self-righteous humility or demanding gratitude.

If he occasionally strutted his power, it wasn't with arrogance but with the self-assurance that came with knowing who he was and what he believed.

Give her a day, two at the most, and she'd be riding

again. She wouldn't hold him up a moment longer than necessary.

She sank back to the blanket and tried to focus on something other than guilt. It didn't help that all she could hear were the sounds of the men readying to leave.

The accusation in Casey's voice nagged at her. Rafe had taken care of her, putting his herd at risk. She wouldn't forget that. Couldn't forget.

Rafe sought out his foreman. "Last time I looked I was still boss of this outfit."

Casey gave him a long look. His already hangdog face dropped into deep folds. "You ain't never missed a roundup, not in all the years I knewed you."

"And I wouldn't now, if I had a choice." But he didn't. Star wasn't able to move. His fault. His responsibility. He kept his voice even, though his heart was anything but. "I need to do this." To assuage the guilt that ate at him.

Casey pulled at his chin. "One of the others can stay."

"If I hadn't pushed her, she'd be all right."

"You didn't know."

"I should have."

"Boy, you can't live your life with shoulds." The foreman's sigh was deep, resigned. "You do what you gotta do. I'll take care of the cattle."

"That's the one thing I am sure of," Rafe said, easy now. He could always count on Casey.

"Take care of her."

"I will."

When Rafe returned, Star was close to tears.

"Hey, princesses don't cry."

"This one does." She sniffled. "I just wanted to show you that I could pull my own weight. Now look at me. I'm practically helpless."

"I thought you had grit."

"I do."

"Then prove it. Let's see how you're doing."

She lifted the blanket, stretched out her leg.

His hands were gentle, at odds with their size, their strength, as they probed her ankle. She shifted her gaze to his face, saw the eyes narrowed in concentration.

She inhaled deeply of his scent, a blend of leather and fresh air, and felt her heartbeat quicken. She needed to steady her breathing. Her heart thudded so loudly, she was certain he must hear its erratic beat.

When he had finished, she pulled the blanket back in place.

"We've got some talking to do," he said.

She nodded jerkily.

"Why didn't you say something?"

"I wanted to prove you were wrong about me."

He nodded, as if conceding the point. "You're one obstinate woman."

She accepted the grudging compliment for what it was.

"Why don't you quit trying so hard?" he asked, trailing a finger down her cheek.

"Old habits."

His gaze raked her face. "Give 'em up."

She wished it were that easy. "When I was growing up, I had to scratch for everything I had. My education. My clothes. Sometimes even the food I put in my mouth."

And she was telling him about her childhood, the grandmother who fed and clothed her out of duty, but withheld the love every child needs.

She was talking too much. She knew it and still she couldn't stop. She'd taught herself to stand firm in the face of childhood memories, to move beyond them. What was there about this man that made her reveal things she'd never told another soul?

"The clothes," he said, understanding dawning in his eyes.

Her head dropped forward, as though in defeat. But when she raised it to meet his gaze, her eyes glittered with defiance. She pointed at the jeans she wore. "I don't wear other people's clothes because that's all I had for too long.

"After my mother died, I wasn't even allowed to keep my name. My mother named me Estrella. Grandmother hated it."

"Estrella. It suits you."

"Not according to my grandmother. After I'd left home, had made . . . gotten my first real job, I went back. I told myself it was time to establish some kind of relationship with her. After all, we were family.

"But mostly I went back because I wanted to show her that I'd made something of myself despite her. Look at me, I wanted to shout. I have pretty clothes, a good job, a happy life."

"What happened?"

Like a roll of film, the scene rewound in Star's mind.

Her grandmother had listened while Star told her of the part in the movie, her mouth pulled into a ruler-straight line. "That's no job for a lady."

"It's not like that," Star said, stung by the mean-spirited words. "It's a real job."

"Do what you must. But don't expect me to take you back."

Star pulled herself from the memories and focused on Rafe's face. "She looked through me, as if I were nothing. Told me to leave. That she didn't love me. Had never loved me. I told myself that nothing had changed, that I shouldn't let it hurt. But it did."

She experienced an odd sense of release as she finished speaking. It was as though some lingering remnants of the hurt and guilt and anger had finally been lifted from her heart.

"You made yourself."

It was exactly what she needed to hear.

She slumped against him, the explanation having taken her last bit of strength. He waited a heartbeat before urging her head onto his shoulder.

She didn't think much about those years, didn't see the need. They were the past. But the past kept creeping into the present. Look at her now. She was practically helpless, because she had been too proud to admit she needed help.

"You're right," she said at last, surprising herself. "I am stubborn."

"That's not always a bad thing," he said.

"I felt like I had something to prove."

"I'd say you've done that."

It was her turn to be surprised.

"Truce?" he asked, holding out his hand.

She put her hand in his. "Truce. You were kind to me last night. Thank—"

"You don't owe me any thanks." The gruffness of the words was in sharp contrast to his earlier kindness. Would she ever understand this man?

She put a hand to her hair and discovered it matted around her face. Unable to sit properly, she struggled with her brush, finally tossing it aside in disgust.

Rafe picked it up and started brushing her hair, the steady strokes soothing. He was a magician, she decided, as she felt the tension drain from her.

She sighed her pleasure. Her head lolled back as he continued brushing.

"That should do it," he said.

He settled a blanket around her shoulders. Her head nestled in the slight dent of his shoulder, and she was aware of only him and the tension humming between them.

Why this man, she wondered. He wasn't her type.

She turned so that her gaze met his. And saw the reason in his eyes.

In another day, she'd be able to travel. Rafe was strangely reluctant to leave this place. These last days with Star had restored a vital part of him, a part he hadn't known was missing.

She joined him. She had an infinite capacity for stillness. She didn't say anything, seeming to understand his need for quiet.

Never had he known a woman so totally attuned to what he was feeling. He realized he was beginning to take such silences for granted. He didn't worry about offending her when he pulled into himself and let his thoughts drift.

He took her hand and brought it to his lips, kissing the center of her palm.

She shivered.

The small convulsive movement made him aware just how vulnerable she was.

He'd seen what a romantic creature she was—her tenderness when she cared for the new calf, her response to a kiss. She was a gentle, emotional woman, who tried very hard not to be.

He looked at her, trying to find defenses against what he was feeling, and failing. His lips found hers. Only a touch, he promised himself, but the kiss deepened.

The kiss was like water, fresh and sweet, after a long day under the desert sun.

Was that her knees going weak, Star wondered. She'd forgotten what a lovely sensation that could be. First, losing herself, then a gathering back. Nerves chased after the heat that rose to her cheeks.

She needed a minute to find her balance, to put a halt to the whirlwind spinning inside her. She raised her gaze to meet his. What she saw there threatened to pitch her world off-kilter once more.

Rafe gave no hint of what he was feeling. His expression remained neutral, even detached.

She didn't have the energy to discern what might lie behind those dark eyes.

The kiss and feelings behind it might not have happened. Had it mattered so little to him, she wondered. She'd poured heart and soul into it.

What really bothered her, though, was how much she found herself caring. How much it hurt that he felt it necessary to put this distance between them.

The woman brave enough to love him would either have to accept the defenses he'd built around her heart—or break her own heart trying to breach them.

Love, the kind of love between a man and a woman that bound them together forever, wasn't likely to be part of the future for herself and Rafe.

Which meant she'd be smart to ignore the attraction she felt for Rafe Mackenzie. She was honest enough to admit that she needed much more from a man than the kind of casual affection where Rafe seemed determined to keep their relationship.

Nothing less than true commitment on every level would satisfy her. A commitment that transcended the physical, reaching the spiritual and emotional highs possible between a man and a woman.

Unless a miracle occurred, she feared Rafe would never be able to give more than a guarded portion of his heart.

"If there's nothing else," she said, "I'd better turn in."

Chapter Five

She'd changed.

Looking back, Star could divide her life into two parts—the city part and now. The city part was full of noise and colors, demands and work. This part, the now, was full of endurance and sweat and partnership. It was an unsettling feeling, one she didn't understand but appreciated nonetheless.

From Rafe, she learned about survival—"When you're looking for water, follow a thirsty coyote"—and about herself. The lessons were all the more valuable because they came from a man who respected both the land and himself.

He showed her how to track. She grew accustomed to eating snake, wild fowl, and rabbit. She'd have plenty of stories to tell her friends when she returned to LA.

The thought caused her heart to hitch with pain. Determinedly, she shoved it aside. The future was still that. The present was all she had, and she intended to hold on to it with both hands.

She learned more about survival, about living off the land, as he taught her how to find water in unexpected places, to distinguish between edible berries and poisonous ones. She popped a handful of dark red berries into her mouth, savored the tart burst of flavor on her tongue. "They're good."

"You bet. Now comes the good part. We play 'let's pretend.'"

The words caught her unaware. She was already playing her own version of that particular game. "Let's pretend?" she repeated cautiously.

"We pretend we have whipped cream, the real kind, not the kind from a can, and shortcake."

"Got it. Strawberry shortcake." She scooped more berries into her mouth, licked her lips, and made a smacking sound. "I can taste it. The whipped cream. The cake. It's perfect."

"Perfect," he agreed, his eyes on hers.

The simplicity of life on the trail made her life in Hollywood seem superficial, even shallow. The trappings she'd surrounded herself with were just that. Trappings. She'd struggled for success for years. Now that she'd earned it, she realized she wanted more.

The dissatisfaction with her job, her life, that had nagged at her for months, had intensified during the days with Rafe. She wanted more from life than a career, no matter how successful it was.

She looked at the man who was becoming more and more important to her. His hair fell across his forehead with casual abandon. She dared to smooth it back.

She wanted love. With Rafe, she believed she'd found it.

Love. That most elusive of all emotions. She had found it in the most unlikely of places. She didn't doubt her feelings. She'd waited a lifetime for this time, this man.

They talked, cautiously at first, more easily as the day wore on. Rafe regaled her with stories about his ancestors. His ties to the land ran deep. A few questions on her part elicited new layers to the man who had turned her life upside down.

As he talked, his drawl grew more pronounced. She wondered if he realized just how thick it had become or how revealing it was. The love in his voice as he talked about his father caused tears to prick her eyes.

She'd never understood families, never known the closeness, the sense of belonging that people bound by love as well as blood enjoyed. She understood duty; her grandmother had drummed it into her with steely determination. But duty didn't equal love. She, better than most, knew that.

He was sharing a part of his life with her, a very important part. She realized that the nature of their relationship had changed. Through a series of circumstances they hadn't chosen, hadn't wanted, they'd become friends.

She needed to tell him who she really was. She knew that he wouldn't take kindly to learning about her profession from another source. So far he'd accepted her explanation that she worked in the media.

Something held her back. If she told him, he'd have yet one more reason to compare her to his ex-fiancee. A woman who'd lied to him, used him, then discarded him.

A puny breeze cooled her skin. They had climbed higher, taking a trail Rafe claimed would bring them closer to the herd in only two days. The terrain had changed accordingly, the ground becoming rougher, the scattering of trees and shrubs growing denser. He pointed out signs of wildlife, cougar tracks, bear droppings, other evidence that they weren't alone.

"Getting tired?" he asked, reining Bear to a halt.

She shook her head. Now that her ankle had healed, she didn't mind the hours in the saddle. The ride was exciting, the country exhilarating, the company . . . well, the company was something she'd have to think about.

A companionable silence settled between them. With only the two of them, they had been forced into an intimacy she'd never have thought possible just a week ago. The thought startled her. Had it been only a week since her car had landed in the gully?

She slanted a glance his way. On horseback, he was a pleasure to watch. He moved as one with the big gelding with a quiet harmony that made her think of her favorite symphony. He was as much a part of his environment as the flat prairie and rugged mountains.

"Up for a little race?" he asked.

At her nod, he pointed to an outcropping of rock. "I'll give you a headstart."

"No way. We'll win on our own." She waited until he gave the signal before tapping Wendy with her heels.

The little mare responded with a whinny, announcing her pleasure at the challenge. Star leaned over her neck and whispered, "We'll show 'em."

Wendy didn't need a second urging.

Rafe and Bear beat them easily, but she didn't mind. The race was just what she needed to clear her mind.

"Not bad for a city girl."

But when he looked at her with those to-die-for dark eyes, she forgot the teasing.

A complex man, Rafe Mackenzie, she thought. A special man. She hadn't felt simple pleasure when he'd kissed her. What she'd experienced was as complicated, convoluted, and confusing as the man himself.

He wouldn't make it easy, for himself or for her. Her lips curved into a smile. She'd always liked a challenge.

Rafe had more sides than a multi-faceted diamond. Warm and giving one moment, cold and remote the next. Too often, he kept her at arm's length as if he was scared of letting her too close.

The idea that he might be afraid caused her to suck

in a sharp breath. The more she thought about it, the more convinced she became that she was right.

It didn't excuse his hot and cold running feelings, but it went a long way to explain them.

Maybe if she found a way to sneak past all those defenses he'd erected, she might find the real Rafe Mackenzie. The glimpses she'd managed to catch of him were enough to convince her the result would be worth the effort.

"Something wrong?" he asked, that quicksilver smile of his nearly destroying her ability to think altogether.

For a moment she saw a man she could love. She shook her head, more in reaction to the unwanted thought than in answer to his question.

"N . . . nothing." Everything. Her world had just been turned upside down. She stared at him, mouth gaping, and wondered if he had an inkling of what she was thinking. Feeling.

For both their sakes, she prayed not.

Everything in her world had gone haywire. She kept looking at him and trying to remember that she'd entrusted her safety to his care, not her heart. But it didn't do any good. The longer she looked, the more she felt herself falling in love. From the moment she'd found him staring down at her in her car, she'd felt weightless, as though her world had suddenly come undone from its anchor. Her heart stuttered.

She wished she could forget how his gaze had moved over her, warm and concerned and admiring.

And she realized she didn't want to forget a thing.

One of nature's miracles pulled her from her thoughts. A doe and her fawn, their subtle colors blending with their surroundings, posed delicately.

"You look happy," he said.

She was. She should have been worried about her long absence. Her agent was probably tearing his hair out, wondering where she was.

None of it mattered.

Rafe gave her one of those patented smiles of his.

She swallowed and tried to remember what they'd been talking about. She wondered if he knew of her feelings for him. The thought caused the color to work its way up her cheeks. Even if he was aware of her blush, he could not possibly know the reason behind it.

Or could he?

Something flickered in his eyes.

She loved him. He'd fight it, she knew. That wouldn't change how she felt. She reached up to lay her hand on his cheek.

She memorized the way he looked at that moment when she realized she loved him. She had no idea where those feelings would lead. For now, she accepted them, embraced them. Love was too rare and precious a gift to reject because of uncertainty or fear of tomorrow.

He took her hand and turned it over to press a kiss in the center of her palm. The tremor that shuddered through her was out of proportion to the simple act. Why this man? Why this time?

His hands settled on the sensitive skin of her upper arms. She shivered tremulously at his touch and felt her stomach muscles contract painfully. He could not possibly be unaware of her reaction, but he gave no notice of it, except to tighten his hold on her ever so slightly.

The setting couldn't be more perfect. Above them, the thin, high clouds turned rose against a turquoise sky. The distant mountains gave fresh meaning to the word majestic. Sage and mustard weed provided splashes of color to brighten the landscape.

The high country held a stark beauty. It wouldn't appeal to all, but it pulled at her. Or maybe it was the man. She couldn't separate the two. Rafe was a part of the land as surely as the jagged rocks and stingy bits of green.

She pointed to a clump of purplish-blue flowers. "What's that?"

"Columbine. Pretty, isn't it?" He pointed to a tiny blossom. "Those are money flowers. Over there, honeysuckle."

She looked closely, saw the twists and coils of honeysuckle twining wherever it could reach.

The land, she decided, could work its way into a person's blood. She wasn't immune to it, she thought, or to him.

He moved toward her, then stilled. He held up a hand when she would have asked what was wrong.

She looked about, searching for the cause of his uneasiness. The landscape appeared as always. Beautiful. Desolate. Deadly.

A screech alerted her they were no longer alone. She looked up to find a mountain lion eyeing them with predatory intent. He looked passive, almost lazy, on his perch on the rock.

"Don't move." Rafe's voice carried to her.

"Don't worry. I'm not going anywhere." Fear rooted her there. She struggled to ignore the light sweat that coated her skin, trickled down her back. It wasn't heat that produced the sweat. It was terror.

She didn't move, though she longed to run. Adrenaline rushed through her blood, and nerves flooded her belly. All the while Rafe kept his gaze locked on her. It was that that gave her the strength to stay put.

Minutes—it seemed hours—passed before the big cat lost interest in them. Her sigh of relief turned into a shaky sob as Rafe gathered her to him.

Embarrassed, she started to back away when his hands settled at her waist, holding her against him. Gradually, she recognized a new sensation growing out of the solid comfort she'd felt while sheltered in his arms. A sensation that had nothing to do with comfort and everything to do with the man who held her.

"It's all right," he murmured. "He's gone."

Her panic slowly subsided, but the need to be close to Rafe, to feel his arms around her, his breath in her hair, only intensified.

She lifted her arms to circle his neck and pressed a kiss to his cheek. "Thank you."

"Hey, if this is the response I get when a cougar comes sniffing around, I owe him one." He skimmed his knuckles across her jaw before his lips closed over hers. They probed, tasting, testing.

She did some tasting of her own. He tasted good. Salty, with the tang of wind and sweat. His mouth was hard, his lips firm, but when they found hers, she felt herself melting. Into them. Into him.

The embrace was nothing like those she shared on-screen. There, it was all about angles, lighting, how it appeared on camera. She didn't worry about the camera now, or angles, or lighting, or anything. Her thoughts were all for Rafe and how he made her feel.

He made her feel just wonderful.

Stars didn't explode inside her head. It wasn't that kind of kiss. It was sweet, almost tentative, asking . . . seeking, for what she wasn't sure.

She gave and, in giving, received. The kiss changed. And then there were stars. Bright, glittering stars that touched something deep inside her. It was every woman's dream. More, it was her dream.

Feeling after feeling flowed through her. Love, so profound that it threatened her equilibrium, not to mention her sanity, poured through her. She reveled in it. In him.

Later, there would be pain. She had no doubt of that, but she determined that there would be no regrets. Rafe deserved better than that. More, she deserved better. Regrets would imply that she'd made a mistake. She wouldn't cheapen what they shared that way.

He reached out to feather his fingers through her hair, sending warm, tingling feelings through her. She lifted her gaze to meet his calm, steady eyes and marveled once again at the strength she read there.

Ribbons of wind whipped around her, causing her to shiver slightly. He pulled her against him, turning her back to him and wrapping his arms around her. She turned in his arms, needing to see his face.

He chucked her under the chin, and her breathing returned to normal.

Rafe watched the play of emotions across her features. Her face was wonderfully expressive. He wondered if she knew just how much of herself she revealed in her eyes. He doubted it. The lady didn't give much away, not if she could help it at any rate.

She not only felt good against him, but right. With some surprise, he realized this was the first time he'd ever known simple contentment in a woman's company. He'd never experienced such peace with Gina. Even in the beginning, there'd been a nervous tension to her, a restlessness that nothing could satisfy, least of all him.

With Star, he felt no such pressure, only a sense of rightness that they should be together. There, with the sunlight in her hair, he kissed her.

* * *

Amethyst shadows dimpled the ground as they set up camp. The thin, dry air had a bite to it, even in late summer. Rafe caught a rabbit in a snare and roasted it over a spit.

Star discovered she wasn't a bit squeamish and prepared to enjoy the meal. Since he cooked, she cleaned up. The division of labor didn't bother her. In fact, the homey act of scrubbing the few dishes brought a certain satisfaction, and she caught herself fantasizing of shared meals and chores and all the rest that went to make up a life together.

They ate by the fire. Hungry as she was, Star never tasted a mouthful of the meal. She was too full of Rafe, and the way he made her feel.

She teetered off the narrow ledge she'd been walking and fell head first into love with him.

Even with the fire, she shivered. The prairie was cold at night. Cold and stark. But there was a beauty to it, in the quiet stillness, the deep blackness relieved only by stars, and the gleam in Rafe's eyes.

"Don't have stars like that in the city, do you?"

It wasn't a question, and she didn't answer, content to simply stare into the night. In LA, the stars didn't stand a chance against the flashing lights and neon glare of a city that never slept. Those visible crowded close to each other, as though they needed to squeeze together to share the limited space.

Here, the stars stretched to cover the expanse of sky.

Each was distinct, a map to those who knew enough to read them.

Rafe would. She knew that, just as she knew he was the kind of man others turned to when they needed help. Hadn't she done just that, instinctively trusting him, even when she had no reason to?

She'd known him less than a week, but he'd impressed himself so deeply in her mind and heart that it was difficult for her to remember how it had been before, when there had been no tall man with midnight eyes who overshadowed every other man she'd ever known.

He had invaded her dreams, in daylight and at night. She was so acutely conscious of him that she heard his slightest breath, felt the stirring of air when he moved.

How did one resist the ache she was experiencing now? The examples of so-called love she'd witnessed in Hollywood had instilled in her the desire to wait until she was sure beyond all reason before taking that step.

She had always suspected that one of the reasons she'd never fallen in love was that so few men lived up to her childhood heroes. Until she found someone who could measure up to that dream man, she was content to devote herself to her career. Now, she knew she'd met someone too compelling to ignore, too annoying to like.

Only once had she'd forgotten her resolve. She'd worked as a waitress during those early days, saving until she had enough to pay for acting lessons. It was there she'd met Alan, an out-of-work actor who praised her talent and professed his love. It was a heady combination for the girl who'd been denied love for so long. He had made her believe, seducing her with promises of forever-after.

When he'd convinced her that he was on the verge of the big break if only he had someone who believed in him, she'd given up the lessons in order to pay for publicity pictures for him. They'd dated for a few months, and she'd believed herself to be in love.

Late one evening, after she'd put in a full day on her feet slinging hash, she'd come home to discover Alan had taken the paltry savings she'd kept in a Mason jar under the sink and left without even a note of goodbye. Even now, her naivete caused her to flush with embarrassment.

She had saved her money, started the lessons again, and gained the attention of her coach. Her first part, a walk-on, had earned her a favorable mention in a review. The roles had grown along with her bank account.

She hadn't looked back.

The leading men who'd played opposite her had never tempted her. Their too-handsome faces left her as unmoved as did their self-involved personalities. She'd endured arranged dates with them for publicity purposes only.

It wasn't that men didn't interest her. It was simply that the kind of men she met in the industry didn't hold her interest. Disappointment seemed an inevitable companion to high expectations. After her first year in Hollywood, she'd decided it was easier, not to mention more entertaining, to stay home with a good book.

She'd been waiting. Until now, she hadn't understood for what. Or whom.

Some of what she was feeling must have shown on her face for he moved closer, taking her hand in his.

The intimacy of the situation hit them both at the same time. Neither spoke nor moved.

She was the first to break eye contact, but it didn't lessen the awareness sparkling between them.

She reached out to caress his face, but her hand shook so badly that she couldn't make her fingers work.

He took her hand in his and laid it against his cheek, a gesture so unexpected, so gentle, that her stomach quivered. Heat skipped along her skin, a physical, tangible force, and impossible to ignore.

He confused her, frustrated her, at times even angered her, and still she wanted him to kiss her. He touched his lips to hers, softly at first.

She lifted her arms to bring him closer. Reason was disregarded, logic ignored.

His lips brushed hers in a feather-light stroke that, nevertheless, had her trembling. She'd known a man's kisses before. So why did this one—this man—leave her so shaken? Tenderness, as sweet as the lips that had touched hers, unfurled within her.

She wanted this. It felt right, so very right. He rested

his hands at her sides. When the kiss ended, she gulped for air and tried to remember her name.

A thumb drifted across her palm, stroking the soft flesh with tiny circular motions that had an unsettling effect upon her. When she surreptitiously tried to withdraw her hand, he smiled and released it, but not before he brought it to his lips and gently kissed each fingertip.

He reached for her other hand, his fingers tightening around her own. The air hummed with tension, an awareness she couldn't deny.

His very look warmed her, and she flushed under the intimacy of it. A slow, sure smile appeared upon his lips, quickening her pulse. She moistened suddenly dry lips and swallowed.

The tip of her tongue was in the corner of her mouth, a gesture he'd noticed she made when she was thinking about something. He stared in fascination. It seemed that the slightest little thing about her snared his attention.

The direction of his thoughts caused him to frown.

"Everything all right?" she asked, startling him and nearly causing him to tip over in his chair.

"What . . . uh . . . sure. Fine."

"You looked like something was troubling you."

Only you. But he couldn't tell her that. He cleared his throat of the lump that had taken residence there.

His thoughts segued to his ex-fiancee.

Gina had been a beautiful woman, demanding his attention and that of every other man with whom she came in contact. He'd tried to tease her out of it, but her demands—and her flirtations—had grown.

They'd festered inside of him, eventually destroying the love that had once burned so brightly. Still, he'd been determined to make the relationship work. Until the day she'd told him she was leaving him for his best friend.

The memory of the bitter words they'd hurled at each other that last day continued to eat away at him. He feared he would carry the guilt with him for an eternity.

Love had taken him for a hard ride once before. He had no intention of getting on that particular horse again, but that didn't mean he and Star couldn't be friends. She had her life; he had his. There was no danger of either of them falling into the trap of love.

For a moment, only a moment, he allowed himself to fantasize of a future with Star. Slowly, he shook his head, dispelling the image. He'd learned the hard way that a city-bred woman could never accept the reality of ranch life.

Ranching was a twenty-four-hours-a-day, three-hundred-sixty-five-day-a-year job. There were no paid vacations, benefit packages, or any other perks except the satisfaction a man found from looking out upon his own land and knowing all that he saw was his.

He loved the land the way other men loved a woman. Totally. Completely. Some might say obsessively. Every year his blood thrilled when it, the land, gave birth once more. Each season brought new delights, bursting in summer, resting during fall and winter, and, in spring, hungry for what he would pour into it.

His pride in it, duty to it, had always been, would always be, the hallmark of his life.

Unbidden, his pa's words came back in a rush.

"Ranching's a tough business. We get up at hard-dark and don't hit the sack again until we're so tired it don't make no difference. But it's what we are. It's who we are. We can no more turn our backs on it than we can walk away from our own skin. There'll be times when you're up to your armpits in manure and wonder why you don't shuck the whole thing." Weak from cancer, he'd been unable to go on.

Rafe had no trouble finishing what his father had wanted to say: Don't give up the land. It's your legacy. And your children's. Hold on to it at all cost.

Mackenzies had worked the land for well over a hundred years—his pa, his pa before him, the one before him. It was as much a part of him as was the Cheyenne blood that ran through his veins.

He'd grown up on stories of how his great-great grandfather, Angus Mackenzie, had arrived in Wyoming from the old country with only the clothes on his back and a need to make something of himself. He'd set his eye on a Cheyenne maiden and kidnapped her.

The girl's father, the old chief, had captured Angus, told him that if he wanted his daughter, he must prove his worth. Angus had taken up the challenge, fighting a Cheyenne brave. And winning. The chief had given Angus his daughter and a stretch of land.

Twenty years later, bureaucrats had tried to take the land from Angus, but by that time he'd become a force in the territory and had held onto what was his.

The land was everything.

Caring for it was Rafe's heritage, and his charge.

His pa had made that clear. What he hadn't made clear was how to hold on to the land when taxes doubled every year and profits continued to drop. Three bad seasons in a row had reduced the ranch's cash flow to a trickle.

Developers, citified vultures with three-piece suits and slicked-back hair, had their eye on the Heartsong. One had offered Rafe top dollar for the ranch. It shamed him, but he'd been tempted. Sorely tempted.

A couple of his neighbors had succumbed to the lure of quick money. He didn't blame them for cutting their losses and getting out, but he wouldn't be doing the same.

The land was part of him, his link to the past, his passport to the future.

He'd fallen for a city girl once before. He couldn't afford to make the same mistake again.

Ranching was the only life he'd ever known, the only one he'd ever wanted. Suddenly, though, that life sounded bleak. He pushed away the thought.

His path had been chosen before he was born.

Chapter Six

Morning came in a burst of light. The sun streamed rich and gold.

Rafe heard Star shift in her sleeping bag. He smiled as she burrowed deeper into its cocooning warmth. He settled into an appreciation of how lovely she was, how totally feminine. Even in sleep, she managed to look beautiful.

Until last night, he'd been certain he could walk away from her without any emotional damage. Now he knew he'd only been fooling himself.

No woman, not even Gina, had ever captured his senses so completely, so utterly. What he felt for Star went beyond physical attraction to genuine caring and respect. He wanted all of her, her mind and her soul.

And her heart? Did he want that as well?

Her sigh purred through the still morning air, and she stirred. He brushed a finger down her cheek.

She swatted his hand away.

He did it again, his smile widening at the annoyed noise she made. "Time to get up, sleepyhead."

"Go 'way," she mumbled.

By that time, the sun was high in the sky. He was grinning for no good reason other than he was happy. Sharing the breakfast chores came naturally, and they squabbled good-naturedly over the cleaning-up.

He cleaned out the frying pan with sand, the grit acting as nature's own scrub brush.

"You do that like you've been doing it all your life," Star said.

"Just about."

Their supplies were running low, but he expected them to reach the main camp within two days. Not entirely unexpectedly, the thought failed to cheer him.

"Rafe, look," Star cried.

A bear cub ambled toward them.

"Don't get too friendly." The warning came automatically. Where there was a cub, a mama bear was nearby. Most likely, an angry mama. "Go on, fellow. Get outta here."

He shooed the cub away, ignoring its attempts to play, but the little animal was persistent. Rafe felt a grin pull at his lips at the cub's antics. He took a careful look around, then relaxed when he didn't spot the mother.

Star held out her hand, laughing when the cub licked it curiously. She was having the time of her life. He could see it in her eyes, hear it in her voice. The cub swatted her with its paw. She sidestepped, chuckled.

The rich sound worked its way through him, reminding him that laughter had been in short supply in his life lately. He joined in, for the sheer pleasure of it.

Still, it wasn't safe to encourage the animal, so he sent the cub on its way.

Rafe packed supplies in his saddlebags, made a final sweep of the area, and prepared to leave. Only Star's pack remained. He frowned as he noticed an unnatural stillness in the air. The normally noisy birds had quieted. Bear tossed his head from side to side.

Star tried to quiet Wendy as the mare shuffled uneasily. "What's going on?"

Rafe held up a hand for quiet. A humming buzzed in his ears.

The gelding reared, the sharp whinny snapping Rafe to attention. Eyes narrowed, he looked about. He didn't hear anything, but he sensed it.

Danger.

Bear took off. Star's mare followed.

The tiny hairs on the back of Rafe's neck prickled. Although he couldn't identify what had spooked the horses, he felt it, a tightening in his gut he'd learned not to ignore. Adrenaline surged through him as the sense of danger grew.

A predator was watching. Waiting.

Careful to keep his movements slow, he turned, scanning the rocks and scraggly trees. Every fiber in him tingled with the urge to move, to act. Whatever was out there, he didn't want to spook it. Sweat formed above his lip, but he couldn't spare the concentration to wipe it off.

His nose twitched. A rancher depended upon his sense of smell for a great many things. A sick cow, fresh blood from a coyote kill, an experienced rancher could detect both and a score of other scents as well. It was part of the survival process.

This time it came too late. The quiet should have tipped him off sooner that something was wrong, but he'd been too tangled up in his feelings about Star to listen to his instincts.

The bear came out of nowhere. She charged them, her tiny eyes bright with a feral gleam.

Rafe yanked Star behind him. "Get out of here."

The bear was on him then, a massive bundle of fury and pure mean.

He spun, taking the brunt of the attack on his shoulder rather than his chest. Her claws scraped down his arm, leaving the mauled skin and exposed muscle screaming with pain—black, greasy waves of it. Screams ripped through his mind.

He wasn't given time to regroup. She attacked again. This time, he wasn't able to avoid the frontal attack. Her claws raked his chest, shredding the denim jacket and shirt to the skin beneath.

He felt like he was on fire. The pain chopped him off at the knees, and he struggled to remain upright. He heard a moan and recognized it as his own.

His knife. If only he could get to it. Already he was losing blood. Too much. He had only a few minutes more before he blacked out.

Somehow he managed to reach inside his boot and pull the knife from its sheath. It was in his hand, poised.

When she came at him, he was ready. He managed to get the knife past her claws and into her middle. That only enraged her further. Fear lent him strength, and he plunged the knife farther into her belly. It strained, the blade angling as he forced it still deeper.

He knew he'd lose consciousness in another minute. Only the thought of Star kept him from passing out. She wouldn't stand a chance against the grizzly. He prayed she'd run when she had the chance. As for himself, well, he'd seen men mauled by a bear. Death usually came slowly. And painfully.

He'd reckoned without Star.

She came at the bear, branch in hand, and began clubbing the animal, a puny David battling a ferocious Goliath. He stared at the slip of a woman holding off the six-hundred-pound bear. She wielded the branch awkwardly, swinging back and then slicing forward. Rafe wanted to laugh at the look of comical surprise in the bear's eyes.

The animal took a swipe at her. He winced as he

saw the claws scrape her arm. Her shirt offered scant protection.

The next minutes passed in a blur, and he wasn't sure if he'd imagined the whole thing. Shock had numbed his brain, and slowed his thinking to a snail's pace.

He tried to yell at her, to tell her to get out while she still could, but his voice was barely a croak. He'd never been much of a praying man. Now he prayed. Time seemed to collapse upon itself as he watched the uneven battle.

He heard someone yelling. Not until he managed to get to his feet did he realize that it was him.

Star landed a blow to the animal's nose. The bear gave a final swipe of a huge paw and then lumbered off, cub trotting gamely behind her.

Rafe's vision had blurred, images swimming before his eyes. Delirious, he thought. He was definitely delirious. Star, with her generous smile and sassy tongue, hadn't just fought off a grizzly. No way. She was Beverly Hills and Rodeo Drive, acrylic nails and designer clothes.

He hadn't finished the thought before he blacked out. Minutes, or was it hours, passed. He wasn't sure of anything, he thought groggily when he came to.

Except the pain.

It choked him, destroying all thought, all reason. It became his only reality, filling his chest, smothering him. Breathing became a battle as he struggled for every gasp of air.

The sound of a voice drifted to him. He tried to focus on it, found that he couldn't.

Shock took over.

The oblivion from which he'd so recently returned beckoned, enticing him to leave behind the fight to remain conscious. It took every ounce of will to keep from slipping back into the darkness, to give up, to admit defeat. He struggled to remember that defeat equaled death.

His own. Star's.

He fought his way through the red mist. The clearing beyond it must exist. For a minute, he wondered if reaching it was worth the struggle, but something in the past was so horrifying that it pressed him forward. What . . . ?

The bear. That was it. Relief that he could remember was short-lived as the agony returned. His shoulder burned where her claws had scored flesh and muscle, ripping each as easily as a child might tear open a piece of candy.

When the pain had filled every cell of his being, he screwed his eyes shut and braced himself against the next wave of it, breathing through his teeth.

Though it took every bit of strength he had, he turned his head, a fraction of an inch only. She was there. The relief that swamped him was nearly as overwhelming as the pain.

When he didn't think he could bear it another second, a blessed numbness took over, giving him a respite. A voice droned in the distance, an insistent buzz that wouldn't go away. He did his best to block it out. He didn't want to return from the blackness that had engulfed him. There, he didn't have to deal with the agony of ruined skin, torn muscle.

"Rafe, can you hear me?"

It was Star who held him, but he was trapped in agony. He was cold, so cold.

She said his name, over and over, pressing him close as if that would bring the warmth back to his body. The pain had him by the throat, pinching all the air from his lungs. He fought it, gasping for his next breath like a man drowning.

He fixed on the sound of her voice, using it to pull him from the quicksand of darkness that engulfed him. He tried to answer, tried to get his tongue around the words, but only a feeble grunt emerged.

"Rafe. Please." The urgency in the voice finally penetrated the fog that coated his mind. Something that sounded like a sob filled the air. He felt his mind start to drift again, struggled to snap it back into clarity.

"Rafe." Her voice seemed to come from a distance. "Rafe!"

The panic in the words punched through the thick haze of pain, excruciating, blinding. He was grateful for it. The shock had numbed him so that he couldn't concentrate. The pain cut through it.

He used it now, tried to focus. Failed, then tried

again. "Star . . ." He heard a moan, took a moment to realize that it had come from him.

The coppery tang of blood coated his mouth. He swiped at it with the back of his hand, smearing the blood. He tried to swallow to rid himself of the taste.

Star used her shirt tail to staunch the flow of blood. "Please, you have to get up. We've got to get out of here. Before she comes back."

Rafe managed to get his brain around the words. She was right. Once the animal had time to recover from the blow Star had delivered, she'd likely be back. And in a temper. She'd been playing with him before. Compared to a grizzly that size, his knife was but a child's toy.

Bears could smell blood, were attracted to the sweet scent of it. He was leaving a steady stream of it.

Still, he didn't move, and Star shook him roughly. "Rafe."

He focused on her eyes. They were dark, determined, but he could see the fear riding in them. Fear for him.

He got his breath back . . . just barely. His lungs burned as he forced himself to his feet. The world spun as nausea and pain stirred in a nasty brew that nearly brought him to his knees. He swallowed back a curse. Whatever energy he could muster was too precious to waste.

Relief slid through her. He could hear it in her sigh.

"Hold on to me," Star said, slipping a shoulder beneath his arm. She slid an arm around him and grabbed hold of the waistband of his jeans. She barely came to his chin, but there was surprising strength in that slender body.

"Too heavy," he said in a slurred voice.

"Put your arm around me."

If he could have managed it, he'd have laughed at the idea of Star supporting him. Right now, he was too weak to appreciate the humor of the situation.

She pulled and pushed and prodded. He latched on to her determination, using it in place of his own.

They stumbled away from the place of the attack. He was bleeding heavily. They'd have to stop and deal with that, as soon as he thought it safe. Trouble was, he wasn't thinking at all. It required too much effort.

When they'd gone as far as he could manage, he motioned to her to stop. She helped him to the ground, careful of his injuries.

He slumped against her, closed his eyes, and felt himself drift. It felt good. So good. A warm pool of darkness, a place he could drown in and forget the pain.

A moan was trapped in his mind, low and long. He tried to swallow around it, found it took too much effort, and gave it up. Deliberately, he forced himself back from the blessed void of unconsciousness that enticed him.

"You saved my life." His voice felt rough as pine bark and twice as scratchy.

"Looks like we're even."

"For a princess, you did good back there," he said

after long moments had passed. He found he could smile, despite the pain.

"We were lucky." Her breath came in short puffs.

"The Cheyenne would say you have a debt on me."

"We all have a debt on each other."

He looked at her curiously. "You really believe that, don't you?"

"You . . . me . . . we all depend on each other."

"The old 'no man is an island' thing."

She didn't have the energy to nod. "That's one way of putting it."

The sound of her own voice calmed her. Deliberately, she slowed her breathing, trying to steady the nerves that sang with terror.

"You all right?" he asked.

"Fine."

The lie slipped easily from her lips. How could she possibly be fine? Rafe had just been savaged by a bear, a bear that could return any moment, full of fury and fresh energy. She had no idea of the extent of his wounds or how to treat them if she did know. Her own arm throbbed where the bear had swiped her.

She tore the remaining sleeve of her shirt into a strip and wrapped it around the scored flesh.

Goosebumps puckered her skin, and she hugged her arms to her. She felt the panicked thunder of her heart, knew she was in danger of going into shock herself.

Rafe had slipped back into unconsciousness. She shook him gently. She couldn't save them without his help. A fresh frisson of fear roiled through her. What if he never regained consciousness?

"Rafe." The urgency in her voice must have gotten through, for he opened his eyes briefly. They were unfocused as he stared at something only he could see. She brushed a finger down his cheek.

"I'm here." Two words, but she clung to them. His jaw tightened, and he was breathing through his nose.

She recognized the signs of shock. Tears fell like rain, dampening her cheeks, though she scarcely registered them.

"Hey, none of that." He lifted his hand to her face.

She took courage from that. "You're bleeding." There was fear in her voice. She hated it, hated the weakness in betraying it. She drew a breath. Another. More steady, she said, "Tell me what to do."

"Got to stop it."

"How?"

"Find some healing herbs." The waver in his voice had grown.

"Tell me what to look for."

She heard the panic in her voice, the fear she tried so hard to hide.

With a grunt, he got to his feet. "I have to show you."

She slipped her shoulder beneath his arm, nearly staggering under his weight. He made an effort to straighten and only succeeded in slumping further on to her.

Hadn't she read some place that fear gave an extra

boost of strength? She gritted her teeth and prayed her adrenaline had kicked into overdrive.

Painstakingly, they picked their way over the rough ground. "What about this?" she asked, gesturing to a small, three-leafed plant.

He sent her a wry look. "I thought you were trying to keep me alive? That stuff'll kill me in ten seconds."

She shuddered.

"Here." He pointed to a tiny flowering shrub. "Get a few of these."

"What's that?"

"Valerian root."

"What does it do?"

"Prevents infection."

She started to yank the plants from the ground.

"Careful. You want to make sure you get the whole plant. Especially the leaves. Brew them into tea."

More gently, she pulled the tiny plants free, shaking the dirt from them. "What next?"

"Start a fire. Boil some water and add the leaves." The lines in his face grew more pronounced as fatigue and pain took their toll.

She worked quickly. Under his watchful eye, she started a fire and put on a small pot to boil, grateful they still had her saddlebags and canteen.

"We need bandages."

She rummaged through her belongings and came up with the silk blouse she'd worn the day he found her. She tore it into strips, her hands clumsy with fear.

Rafe gave a weak smile. "That's the fanciest bandage I've ever seen."

Her teeth were chattering, so she clamped her lips together.

"Put in the strips."

She wrinkled her nose as she stirred the brew. "That is one wicked smell." She lifted the makeshift bandages from the steaming pot with a stick.

She helped him remove his jacket, then peeled away his shredded shirt. Angry gashes scored his chest.

"Rafe—"

"It's worse than it looks," he said with a weak attempt at humor.

Sickness slicked her insides, chilled her bones.

"It's all right." The words were so slurred she could barely make them out.

Hands slippery with blood, she laid the bandages across his chest, knowing the pain she was inflicting and knowing she had no choice. It didn't keep the tears from tracking down her cheeks.

She repeated the words to a prayer from long ago, the child-like words balm to her terror-ridden mind.

Rafe opened his eyes and focused on Star's face. Sweat and blood and tears marked her cheeks. She was murmuring something that sounded like a prayer. Silently, he added his own plea for help from above.

His admiration for her grew. She had just fought off a bear, endured a grueling trek while bearing most of his weight, and tended wounds that would have sent most women into hysterics, but her worry was for him.

Fear shadowed her eyes, but her mouth was firm in determination. Her hands were shaking by the time she finished, but she had kept her head. The lady had more than her share of pluck. Beneath that pretty exterior lay a steel core, one he was only beginning to comprehend.

She helped him to stand. "Which way?"

He struggled to remain on his feet, fighting the ever-increasing waves of sickness. He forced himself to think clearly . . . or die. "That way," he said, pointing to the distant mountains.

He felt her stiffen and understood. The mountains were at least twenty miles away, an impossible distance given their circumstances. But it represented their only hope.

The mountains had water. Crossing the prairie on foot was suicide. He didn't worry about the horses. Their instincts would lead them to water and eventually back to the ranch. Right now, they stood a lot better chance than he and Star did.

He concentrated on putting one foot in front of the other. Even with Star taking most of his weight, he scarcely had the strength to keep moving. His world had narrowed to that one objective. Putting one foot in front of the other.

One step at a time. One breath at a time.

His breathing grew more labored. At first, he tried to

hide it from Star. After a while, he gave it up. He wasn't fooling her.

Through it all, Star was there. The quiet strength in her eyes didn't falter, though he knew she was terrified. It was but one more sign of her courage. Her determination forced him to use his legs when he wasn't sure he remembered how.

He slipped on a loose rock and stumbled. Star tried to break his fall, but they landed heavily on the unyielding ground. She took the brunt of it. He could hear the breath whoosh from her.

He wondered if he could get to his feet again, and couldn't find it in him to care. He was fading rapidly. His strength was gone, his energy spent. He drew deep within himself to scrape together another burst.

"Why didn't you get out of here when I told you to?"

She didn't bother answering.

Silently, he berated himself. He'd snapped at her when she'd put her life on the line to save his. "You need to go." Each word cost him. "Staying here's only going to get both of us dead." It was guilt as much as temper that rippled through him.

"No way, cowboy. Now get to your feet or I'm gonna kick you from here to LA."

He focused long enough to take in the set of her jaw. "You would, wouldn't you?"

"You bet I would."

It didn't matter that he could scarcely see her face through the murk of pain. It didn't matter that the bear's attack had squeezed most of the life from him. None of it mattered. Only Star.

Her smile wobbled around the edges, but it was there. She was one gutsy lady. "Time's up."

He could all but hear her gritting her teeth as she got to her feet. He was doing some gritting of his own. The brief rest had only reminded him how weak he was, and getting weaker by the minute. He was a liability, to himself and to her.

They started walking. Limping was more like it, he thought, as they scrabbled over the rough terrain. She was tiring; he heard it in her breathing, felt it in the brace of her body as she took more and more of his weight.

He felt compelled to try again. "This isn't working."

"It's all we have." This time, she sounded more resigned than determined, though.

He didn't waste energy arguing. He put himself on automatic. Didn't think. Didn't feel. Didn't wonder how much longer they could keep going. If he did, he was afraid he'd come to his senses and realize there was no way they could make the twenty or so miles they had to cover.

Twenty miles in this terrain was a good piece when you had a horse, supplies, and a body that wasn't broken and bleeding. Given that they had next to nothing in the way of provisions and he was worse than useless, it was an impossible distance.

Star didn't give him the luxury of giving up. She

ordered, bullied, cajoled, threatened, and when those no longer worked, she cried. He could withstand any of the rest, but he couldn't hold out against her tears.

A man would have to be made of stone to resist them. He suspected she knew it. He didn't care. She had gotten them this far by sheer grit. It hit him with humbling awareness that she had more courage than he did.

A lone raven screamed above—the legendary bird of death and darkness. He wondered if it was an omen. The depressing downward spiral of his thoughts dragged at him. He shook it off. He couldn't afford the negative energy.

Once they stopped for the night, she rebandaged his wounds.

Having a woman wait on him grated. "I can do it."

"Don't be stubborn."

"Old habit," he said, remembering a similar conservation. Had it been less than a week ago?

"Give it up."

He wished it were that easy. He'd been raised to protect women, to shield them from the harsher parts of life. When he failed at that, he failed as a man. The acknowledgment left a bitter taste in his mouth, and a smear on his conscience.

He knew it was chauvinistic of him, but he had never willingly let a woman take care of him. He'd be the first to admit that women were equally capable, equally intelligent as men, but training and nature made him feel responsible.

He could barely drag himself off to relieve himself away from camp. So how was he going to take care of Star?

The answer was simple. He wasn't. He was dependent upon her for everything. The knowledge trampled upon his pride.

She laid a hand on his cheek. "We've got a long day tomorrow. You need to rest."

She didn't move, and he watched as exhaustion slipped across her features. Tomorrow they'd both need every ounce of energy and strength they could muster. With that in mind, he took Star's advice and fell off the edge of fatigue. He fell asleep watching her watching him.

Star heard Rafe breathing slow and was grateful he could sleep. She didn't sleep, couldn't afford to.

Was it only a day, two days ago, that she'd believed she had sorted through what was important for survival? Their horses, tents, and sleeping bags were gone. She now had only her determination to get them out of this.

Her priorities had shifted. Again. Keeping Rafe alive was the only thing that mattered.

His fever worsened during the night. Sweat coated his face, yet he shivered convulsively. Fear flowed from her pores in a sweat that stank of terror. Not for herself, but for Rafe.

Panic rose sickly from her gut to her throat.

To warm him, she wrapped her arms around him and

held on. They stayed there, locked together, throughout the night.

The rasp of his breathing lulled her, threatening her self-imposed vigil, but she forced herself to stay awake. Their survival depended upon her.

The knowledge was enough to keep her eyes open, and her heart pounding. She'd played the heroine in a dozen movies, managing to triumph over outlaws, snakebite, and tornados. Then, she'd had topnotch writers to get her out of any predicament, no matter how dire. She had no one but herself to rely upon now.

It was a daunting thought.

Once more, she began to pray.

Chapter Seven

The night's dark began to soften and thin. Rafe woke slowly, his brain thick and gummy, like cold syrup. He pushed his way through it, trying to fix on the words floating in the air. He managed to grab a few.

". . . are you . . ."

The words faded as the pain took over. It was a living thing, consuming him and everything around him. He was steeped in it.

He fought his way out of it and the panic that came with it. His entire body ached like an open wound, which wasn't far from the truth. The bear had managed to rake his chest and arm with her flesh-tearing claws. He supposed he ought to count himself lucky she hadn't had time to start on his face.

"Rafe?"

Star's voice. The normal honeyed tones were hoarse and raspy.

"Hi." The word came out as a croak.

She smiled faintly. "Hi, yourself. How're you feeling?"

He grimaced.

"Stupid question, right?"

He settled for a nod, then wished he hadn't. "I feel like a rattler had me for dinner." His voice was rough. He hoped she knew it wasn't for her.

"Okay, you're feeling lousy." She reached for his hand and tightened her fingers around his. Her voice was thick with exhaustion, and he realized she hadn't slept.

"How . . . how long?"

"Twelve hours. Maybe more."

Twelve hours. He looked around. "Where are we?"

She gave a small shrug. "Somewhere away from the bear."

"How did we get here?"

"We walked."

He knew he hadn't walked, at least not without a lot of help. His disbelief must have shown in his face, for she said, "It was a mutual effort."

He doubted that. He'd been nearly delirious. He outweighed her by at least sixty pounds. "You carried me." Even through the haze of pain, he heard the awe in his voice.

She made a face. "It was more like dragged." She hesitated. "Will your men come looking for us?"

"Probably."

"But—"

"We're not where they're likely to find us."

"I see."

"Most women would have passed panicked hours ago and moved straight to hysterical."

"But, then, I'm not most women."

"No, honey, you surely are not." He pushed the hair back from her face. "You're beautiful."

That surprised a laugh from her, a sound of frayed nerves and tension too long pent-up. "Yeah, right. I've been out here for over a week. I smell like something that ought to be shot. I'm really beautiful." Tears trembled in her voice.

Because he needed it, he reached for her hand, linked their fingers. "You could spend a year here and still be the most beautiful woman alive."

Lightly, she swatted his uninjured arm. "Mackenzie, you beat everything. You would choose now to go and give a girl a compliment?" She placed a hand on his forehead, the time-honored method of determining fever. "You must be hurt worse than I thought."

She propped his head up. "Drink."

He sniffed at the cup and recognized valerian. She'd brewed another cup of tea from it.

"You learn fast."

"I'm a quick study."

He drank, scowling as a trickle of the bitter liquid slid down his throat.

"I'll be fine." He didn't believe it.

Neither did she.

"Don't frown. It makes lines." He reached up to smooth the furrows between her brows. "Don't want them marring that pretty face." Pain thickened his voice, and she had to strain to hear the words.

"Lines give a face character." Her own voice was scarcely stronger.

The banter felt good. It took her mind off her worry, if only for a few minutes. Rafe wasn't any better. If anything he was worse.

She was scarcely better off. Her eyes burned from lack of sleep, her stomach raw from bile and fear. Her arm throbbed. She calculated it had been twenty-four hours since they'd had anything to eat.

She kept her smile bright and her worry to herself. She brewed another pot of the tea, helping him up so that he could drink it. He managed only a few sips before slumping back in her arms.

"You're looking better," she said.

"Liar."

Her nod was silent acknowledgement of the charge. That didn't mean she was going to give up.

"You've got to go." His voice sliced out, and she flinched as though struck. "Get out of here while you still can. No sense both of us . . ."

She understood what he didn't say, and why. Outrage gave her strength. She'd need that and more. "I won't let you die. I won't let you die! I love you, you big, dumb cowboy. You hear that? I love you."

"If you love me, get out of here. You've got a chance without me."

"You're two cows short of a roundup if you think I'm letting you get away with that crap."

"Steers," he murmured weakly. The ghost of a smile flirted with his lips.

"Steers, cows, what's the difference? I don't see any bulls around at the moment." She was talking nonsense, anything to keep the fear at bay. "What's the matter? Afraid a city woman is going to show you up?"

"The day you can outdo me, honey, is the day I eat my boots." His voice was but a shadow of its usual self, but she took strength from his attempt to respond to her teasing.

She cast a glance at his scuffed boots. "They look chewy, but then you like your meat tough and stringy, don't you? Like those steers of yours."

That earned a chuckle from him.

"Quit your talking and start walking," she said. "We've got a lot of miles to cover today."

They headed out. When she faltered under his weight, he pushed away from her, steadying himself with an effort.

Star gritted her teeth and wrapped an arm around his waist. She ignored the constant ache in her shoulders, the burn of over-burdened muscles. A line of sweat trickled down her back. She ignored the cramp in her legs. She ignored everything but the need to get Rafe to shelter.

When he fell and resisted her efforts to get him back to his feet, she goaded him. Sympathy could kill them both. If she couldn't motivate him, she figured she'd make him mad. "You're like those mangy animals of yours. Lazy and good-for-nothing."

His eyes narrowed until he suddenly laughed. "You're good, princess."

"You best remember that."

"That's my girl." Affection layered the words beneath the pain.

She caught a glimpse of a grin. It made her wince to see the lines of suffering even that small movement caused him.

"We'll get out of this. Or die trying." Too late she realized she'd spoken the words aloud. The melodramatic vow sounded like something from one of the B movies she'd made early in her career.

"Hey, pretty lady, I'm too tough to die."

Beneath their teasing, she was more worried than ever. He'd lost a lot of blood. Too much. His face was gray beneath his tan, and his eyes glazed. If they didn't reach shelter soon, she'd lose him. She knew it as surely as she knew she couldn't let it happen.

Rafe had saved her life. More than once. Now it was her turn. She didn't intend on letting him down. She gritted her teeth. "Come on, cowboy. We're not done yet."

But they would be, she thought, if she didn't do something. Soon.

She concentrated on staying upright. Her back was screaming with the strain of supporting Rafe, and still she kept going. When she stumbled over a rock, she plunged to the ground, taking him with her.

She lay there, panting. At last she stirred herself enough to lay a hand on his cheek. She scanned the area. An outcropping of rocks would provide needed shade.

She pushed herself up, bent from the waist to brace her hands on her thighs, and drew a steadying breath. With an unvoiced prayer, she reached down to help Rafe. They staggered to the stingy bit of shelter. "We'll rest for an hour."

Rafe nodded. It suited him very well. The longer, the better. He had a plan of his own.

He waited until her breathing slowed, then waited until he was certain she had slid into sleep. His injuries made it difficult to move quietly, but he managed it. Too much depended upon his making it far enough away that Star couldn't find him.

It would take a miracle for them to get out of here. A man who made his living from the land didn't put much stock in miracles. He wouldn't drag Star down with him. No sense in both of them dying.

Without him, she stood a chance.

When Star found him gone, she'd understand. Perhaps she'd even be grateful. He left the blanket and canteen. She'd need every advantage if she was to make it out of here alive. With a last lingering look at her, he started off. He made it to a hollowed-out tree, far enough away that she wouldn't easily find him.

The exertion had cost him. The pain reared up, biting him in the arm, the chest, and the belly. His breath came in uneven gasps, even as he worked to smother the ragged puffs.

He huddled inside the rough shelter, grateful for protection from the pitiless sun. Time lost meaning. His thoughts wandered. Maybe he dozed. He couldn't be sure.

Star awoke abruptly, the feeling that something was wrong jolting her from sleep. The quiet was too quiet. She reached for Rafe and found the spot next to her empty.

For a moment, she allowed herself to hope that he'd taken a privacy trip and would return any minute. She knew better, though. A red fury bubbled just under her skin. She welcomed the anger, for it kept the fear at bay.

A quick survey of the area revealed he'd gone farther than she'd believed possible. He must have fought for every step.

If she hadn't been so exhausted. She'd have heard

him. She didn't waste time on self-recriminations. They wouldn't bring Rafe back.

She made a slow search of the area, fanning out in ever larger circles. She continued until she realized she was only exhausting herself, using precious energy she couldn't afford.

"I'm not leaving you," she shouted into the silence. "The longer you make me look for you, the longer it'll be before we reach help."

She waited. All she heard was her own voice. Too shrill. Too frightened. She made a show of dropping to the ground, stretching her legs, a casual pose as though she had nothing more on her mind than her next manicure.

Silence stretched around her, until a string of weary grunts had her turning in that direction.

Rafe stood, face gray, eyes resigned. He made a sound that might have been frustration, might have been anger, or a combination of the two. "You could give a three-legged mule lessons in stubbornness."

They were the most beautiful words she'd ever heard.

She was too relieved to be furious. She reached him, only to be warned away by a shake of his head.

"Why didn't you leave? We can't make it, but you can. If you leave now. Stay and you'll kill any chance we have. You'll find the main camp if you keep heading west. Send back help."

She wasn't deceived. He was giving her the chance to live, and killing his own. "We're going to make it. Together. You can count on it."

Brave words, she thought. How was she going to make good on them? Rafe's life depended upon her. Only her. That steadied her as nothing else could have.

They headed back to where they'd left their supplies. Without speaking, she gathered them up, then turned to slip her shoulder beneath Rafe's arm. Resolutely, they started walking.

Her feet felt like they were disappearing into sand. Lifting them—first one, then the other—took every bit of energy she possessed.

She didn't need to look at Rafe's face to know he was at the end of his endurance. His breathing grew harsher with each step. Pain shimmered through the fatigue written on every line of his face.

She took more and more of his weight, trying to keep them both upright. More than once, she wanted to stop, to call a halt to the madness that made her think she could get them out of what felt more and more like a death march.

When she spotted the cabin, she wondered if she was hallucinating. A cabin in the middle of nowhere. If she could have dredged up the energy, she'd have rubbed her eyes with her free hand. Instead, she shook Rafe lightly. "Look."

He didn't respond.

Hallucination or not, she was heading to it. She all

but dragged him the remaining steps. The door felt reassuringly solid against her hand as she pushed it open.

The cabin with its log walls and scrapboard floor was more primitive than rustic. The two cots didn't promise comfort. The whole place smelled stale with disuse.

It looked like a palace to her.

The first order of business was to make Rafe as comfortable as possible. She checked his bandages, relieved to find them dry. The bleeding had stopped. She sniffed cautiously and decided she didn't smell infection.

Once she settled Rafe on a narrow cot, she checked out their temporary home. A wood-burning stove occupied one corner. Cabinets topped it. Hardly daring to hope, she opened a door and found canned goods. No suspicious bulges or smells warned her off.

By the time she'd pried open a can with a knife and found two chipped bowls, Rafe was asleep.

She ate half a can of peaches and decided she'd never tasted anything better. The rest, she carefully saved.

She made a trip outside, then returned and studied Rafe. The stubble that prickled his jaw had darkened, stressing the lines bracketing his mouth. Sleep-mussed hair fell across his forehead.

Rafe was alive. That was all that mattered.

Rafe licked syrup from Star's fingers as she fed him peaches from a can. "You taste good."

She rolled her eyes. "It's the peaches."

He shook his head. "No. You."

He managed a trip outside. His strength was returning, slowly but steadily. He still favored his side and walked with a slight limp, but the weakness was gone. The herbal mixture Star had applied to his wounds had prevented infection. All in all, he was a lucky man.

Through it all, Star was there, quietly doing what was necessary, never once complaining.

She had proven herself again and again. It shamed him that he'd once labeled her a spoiled city girl.

"Wipe your feet." She sounded very wifely, Rafe thought. He liked that, despite the face he made at her.

He looked about the cabin with its uneven floor and rough walls.

"It doesn't matter," she said, reading his thoughts. "Just because we're temporarily living in a cabin doesn't mean we can't keep it clean."

She'd made a home here, he thought. A few twigs in a tin can graced the table. She'd swept the floor with a branch. But it was feelings that made a home. Tenderness. Respect. Love.

The word gave him pause.

He recalled her screaming declaration that she loved him. Adrenaline, he'd thought at the time, had prompted it. That and the need to force him to keep going. Now he wondered. Star wasn't the kind of woman to say those words without meaning them. He didn't want the responsibility of love.

"Ma used to chew me out regular for tracking in dirt. I remember when I was twelve, I got my first deer. Came tracking in dirt and blood. She had a fit. Had me scrubbing floors for weeks after."

Star seemed content with puttering around the cabin, making it more hospitable. He didn't feel he had to entertain her, and she didn't pester him with questions about his moods, as Gina had done. His pa would have liked Star, he thought absently.

She wasn't like other women he'd known, always wanting to fill the silence with empty chatter. She simply asked questions.

And more often than not he found himself answering them.

Maybe it was her smile. Maybe it was the way she didn't push. He wasn't sure what it was about her, but he ended up telling her things. About himself. About his life. About his *feelings*.

He told her things he'd never shared with another soul, even Casey, and because he shared the troubles with her, he felt much of the tension slip from him.

Before he'd known what was happening, he'd told her more about his past than he'd ever shared with anyone.

"Tell me more about your father," she said.

He discovered he was eager to talk about the man who had done more than anyone else to shape the man he'd become. A few quiet questions on Star's part started him talking, and remembering.

"Pa was part Scot. He used to joke that he was so

cheap that he could steal the bark from a dog. Truth was, I never knew a more generous man."

Sam Mackenzie had been a good man, honest in his dealings, and so fair that folks had come from miles around to have him settle disputes. Though he'd left school after the eighth grade and had never set foot in a university, people had taken to calling him Judge. He had accepted the name with good nature and even better sense. He'd remained what he was—a simple man with no ambition other than to care for his family and the land entrusted to him.

He'd asked of his son what he demanded of himself, hard work and integrity. That, and respect for the land. Only once had Rafe seen his father cry . . . when he'd had to put down a mare savaged by wolves. Even then, Sam hadn't blamed the wolves or set traps like so many of his neighbors had.

He had done what had to be done and then wept like a child, unashamed of his tears. He and Rafe had stood over the grave for a long time. Rafe learned an important lesson about being a man that day. A man did what he had to, despite the cost to himself, and wasn't ashamed to shed tears when moved.

Sam had been a man of few words, letting his actions speak for him. Helping a neighbor raise a barn, loaning a friend enough money to pay off back taxes, helping his young son through the throes of first love, he'd done each quietly, without fuss or fanfare.

Times changed, and money had dried up due to a

drop in beef and wheat prices. Sam had again done what had to be done, selling off equipment and taking out a second mortgage. When Rafe had asked why he hadn't gone to those same friends for a loan, Sam had replied that he wouldn't put his friends in the position of having to say no.

His sense of humor had kept him going through times that would have felled a lesser man. Even when cancer had taken nearly everything from him, including his dignity, he had kept his sense of humor.

He'd wagged a shaky finger at Rafe and warned, "Don't go trying to put one of those grownup diapers on me. You're not too big for a trip to the woodshed."

Rafe had grinned through his tears and done what had to be done. Disease and the resulting pain had whittled Sam Mackenzie down to a husk of the man he'd once been.

He scrubbed a hand over his face. He hadn't realized so much of that precious time spent caring for his pa was still with him. It took Star and her quiet ways to bring it back.

Only when she put her hand on his did he realize he'd been talking for over an hour. "You loved him very much."

Some of the pain that pinched his heart eased. "You have a gift for listening. For understanding."

"That's probably the nicest thing anyone's ever said to me."

Being with her was both peaceful and exciting. The

contradiction of feelings continued to amaze him, and frustrate him.

She was the first woman in a long time with whom he'd wanted to open his heart. She touched him in a way he was reluctant to define. Because if he did, if he tried to put words to it, he might have to act on them.

What's more, he'd started thinking of the future. A future with Star.

The idea was laughable. Wasn't it?

She should have looked out of place in the rough cabin with its log walls, wood floor, and crude furniture. Even with her hair pulled back in a simple ponytail and no makeup, she was the most beautiful woman he'd ever known. She had an unconscious grace, a natural loveliness that nothing could diminish.

He kept waiting for her to look out of place there. Out of place with him.

But she didn't.

That awareness caused him to look at her with new eyes. She was more than he'd first thought. He thought of his life, a life he wouldn't trade for all the money in the world, but it was a hard one. How would Star handle it, he wondered.

Sure, she'd proved herself on the trail. Over and over. They'd reach civilization soon, though, and what then? Would she look back on the week spent with him as a lark, something to be laughed about over dinner with friends? Or would she feel about the time together as he did?

The self-doubt was unaccustomed. He didn't like it, didn't know what to do about it.

Perhaps that was why he found himself telling her more about Gina and how she died. "I keep wondering if I'd tried harder to make her happy, she'd still be alive."

"You blame yourself." It wasn't a question, but a statement.

He wasn't surprised Star understood what he'd never tried to put into words before. What startled him was the relief he felt upon giving voice to his feelings. He hadn't loved Gina in a long time, but he'd never wished her ill. It was guilt that gnawed at him, not rejection.

Star laid a hand on his arm. "Believing you can control everything that happens—good and bad—is a kind of arrogance. Gina made her own choices. We all do. Life is full of what-ifs. Don't torment yourself with them."

He was no longer amazed by her perception. Somewhere along the way he had come to accept the fact that she knew him better than he did himself. The knowledge, unsettling at first, now warmed him. No one, not even his father, had so fully understood him.

His feelings were no longer his own. At one time, he'd have resented that. With Star, though, he accepted it, savoring the knowledge that he was not alone.

With the firelight stroking her hair and skin, she looked soft and delicate. She'd proved that she was anything but. The woman who had fought off a bear and dragged him to safety had more steel in her backbone than most men he knew.

He caught the faint whiff of wood smoke and the scent of pine.

It was a moment caught in time, one he knew he would remember for the rest of his life. Years could slip by and he would remember her just as she was now.

There were infinite shadings to this woman, and he wanted to know them all.

He wanted to remember her as she was now, lips slightly parted, eyes soft and dreamy. He knew how she would feel if he touched her. But he wouldn't touch her—not yet. Right now, he wanted only to absorb this one moment.

He didn't trust himself to speak. A word might shatter the mood. He was loathe to do anything, say anything, that might destroy the fragile state of feelings.

He frowned. She'd lost weight during the last week. He could span her waist with two hands and have room to spare.

"Star." He hadn't meant to say her name aloud, had meant only to whisper it, but he'd needed to hear the sound of her name on his lips.

He didn't try to sleep, wanting to savor these hours with her. He didn't mind his wakefulness. It gave him the opportunity to watch her. Firelight bathed her in gold, cast intriguing shadows across her face, highlighting the line of her cheekbone, the softness of her lips.

She was peaceful in sleep, a fist tucked under her chin as a child might. The energy that was so much a part of her was absent now.

Her deep breathing told him she was exhausted. Who could blame her? She'd been taking care of him.

He stood, wincing as his bare feet hit the cold floor. He went to the fire, stirring the dying embers to life. A burst of heat hit him. He savored the warmth, rubbing his hands together.

He turned back to stare at Star. As always, he was mesmerized by her beauty. She needed sleep. He could use a few hours as well, but his mind was churning.

In a few days, they'd cover the last miles. She'd return to her life in Los Angeles and he, well, he'd head home. The anticipation left him cold inside. Home didn't have the appeal it once did. He didn't like knowing that soon she would no longer be in his life.

He tried to picture himself living in the city. How could anyone prefer the suffocation, he wondered, where a person felt smothered by too many people, too many things. He recalled a recent trip to Laramie. The streets clogged with cars and irate drivers, buildings a garish parody of nature's own skyscraping mountains, houses cramped together with scarcely a slice of sky between them.

He could hardly take a step without bumping into someone. It was a pretty enough city, he'd supposed, if you liked all the noise and confusion. The sheer number of people, where everyone seemed in a desperate rush to get somewhere other than where they were, had made him yearn for the quiet of the ranch and the clean air perfumed by the scent of pines instead of exhaust fumes.

Of course, a city-dweller might see things different-ly, might not feel the tug of the land, the freedom of the open range.

He pictured Star living and working in the city. A woman as beautiful as Star wouldn't be alone. The image of her kissing another man was as vivid as it was unwelcome. He fisted a hand at his side.

How did he live with that? He had no say in her life, especially when he sent her on her way. She was a free agent, with a life of her own, a life far removed from his.

A frown chased across his face as he acknowledged that their days at the cabin were coming to a close. He'd begun to think of it as their own private sanctuary. How could he walk away from her, he wondered.

He wasn't a man who made promises. She hadn't asked for any. Not aloud, at any rate, but it was there in her eyes. She'd said she loved him. He knew she wasn't the type of woman to utter the words easily. That she'd done so to him, for him, moved him unbearably.

He had never needed a woman the way he needed Star. It felt dangerously like love. He couldn't forget those moments when he'd felt she could not only read him but knew him better than anyone else ever had. She wove a spell around him, working her magic until he felt he was drowning in her.

He felt good. More than good. He felt great. He glanced at the woman beside him.

Was he falling in love with her? Had he already fallen? He rubbed a hand over his heart, frowning over the flutter in it.

His jaw tightened. Love had no place in his life. Not any longer. His path had been decided. He wouldn't be changing it now. Not even for a woman as compelling as Star.

Chapter Eight

Star had never known time to speed by as it did at the cabin. They'd spent only two days there, but it seemed like forever. At the same time, it could never be enough.

Location shots usually passed quickly, the excitement of visiting new places, the sheer thrill of the actual shooting, but they didn't compare to the sheer joy she experienced with Rafe, the man she loved.

He grew stronger with every passing hour. While Star was grateful for his recovery, she dreaded the day when they would leave this small slice of paradise.

It was the far edge of summer. Nearly imperceptibly, the days grew shorter, the dark coming sooner than the day before. She hoarded each day, like a miser grasping his cache of gold, unwilling to give up one minute of her time with Rafe.

She began to hoard the minutes, the hours—counting them out and treasuring each as a precious gift. All too soon, they would end.

With each day that passed, she knew she was adding another link to the chain that bound her to Rafe, and to the land. An invisible chain, one forged with memories, both large and small, and, most of all, love.

She hadn't used the word again, knowing instinctively Rafe didn't want to hear it. Instead, she tried to show him how she felt.

She was tied to him. Could it be that everything that had happened in her life had been only to bring her to this time, this man? She wasn't ashamed of her feelings. How could she be, when they had brought her the greatest joy in her life?

A frown wrinkled her brow as a thought struck. The big, tough cowboy was embarrassed by his feelings for her. She'd teach him to accept what was between them. In time, perhaps he'd come to love her as she did him.

Time would tell if what they'd shared on the high plains would strengthen or fade. For herself, she knew. She knew beyond all doubt, all reason, that she and Rafe belonged together.

He was too vital, too everything to make an easy or undemanding companion, but she'd discovered something. She didn't want easy or undemanding. She wanted Rafe. Just as he was. Hard-headed and proud and valiant.

There was something fanciful about this land, where

the clouds dusted the mountains and the sky was so brilliantly blue that it hurt the eyes. Magic touched the land . . . and her feelings for this man. It seemed natural to love him, to share the life he lived.

Rafe belonged here. She could belong too. Already she thought of this small piece of earth as home. She knew if he asked her to stay, she would.

More than ever, she knew that she loved him, but there'd been no mention of the future, of what would happen once they reached civilization.

She reminded herself that they still had a day or two before Rafe could travel. She intended to make the most of them.

She hadn't worried about her hair or makeup in more than a week. Her stylist would no doubt have a fit when he saw her hair. She noticed the ragged state of her nails and grinned. They were a wreck. Without all the demands of her career and public image, she felt free to be herself for the first time in years.

The image required by her work was a twenty-four-hour, seven-day-a-week thing. Even a trip to the grocery store meant full makeup. Battle armor, she called it.

She had grown up. Changed, she thought, for the better. She lifted her gaze. An eagle soared overhead, its wingspan easily five or six feet.

The wild creature swooped, its wings dipping, before climbing once more. Transfixed, she stared. The sky and mountains were no more than a backdrop for the aerial ballet the eagle performed.

"It's beautiful." The words came out as the barest whisper.

"If we wait long enough, we'll see its mate." Rafe's voice broke through her frozen wonder.

Impulsively, she turned to him, started to throw her arms around him before remembering his injuries. Instead, she framed his face with her hands and brushed her lips over his.

Love sparkled through her. It filled her, this feeling for him. How could it not? Love for this man was the most important thing to ever happen to her.

As Rafe predicted, the mate showed up. She imagined she could hear the two of them greeting each other. She watched as the pair performed a *pas de deux* in the sky. Rafe had told her that eagles, like hawks, mated for life. The idea appealed to the romantic in her.

A shiver traced down Star's spine as she recalled those moments when she feared the bear would kill both of them. If not for a bit of luck, it undoubtedly would have. She pushed the frightening pictures away and concentrated on the beauty surrounding her.

The scene was enough to take her breath away. Mountains poked their peaks through low-slung clouds. The clouds themselves were cotton puffs against the bluer-than-blue sky. Sunshine filtered through them, dappling the ground in a crazy quilt of shadow and light.

Rafe was nearly recovered. His healing had been nothing short of a miracle, and she was fiercely grateful for it.

In another day, maybe two, Rafe would be able to travel. She'd come to think of the cabin as home. Never mind the circumstances that had brought them there. It was a haven, both from the elements and from the demands that would beset them when they returned to their respective worlds.

Worlds. Not world, but worlds. For they lived in two separate worlds. Could they make the two of them mesh? The question tormented her.

For too long, she'd always thought in terms of the future. She couldn't afford to take her career for granted, had always felt that she must plan ahead. Now, she had no other plan than to squeeze as much love and laughter as she could in to whatever time was left to them.

They explored their small slice of heaven and found a small stream.

Star didn't wait but kicked off her shoes and waded in up to her knees. The water was frigidly cold, but she welcomed the chance to wash away some of the trail dirt.

She splashed her face with water, not surprised when her hands came away grimy. She must have looked a fright with dirt and who knew what else clinging to her.

They played together like children. Even work became fun when they did it side by side. The most mundane tasks turned into something special when shared with the man she loved.

Tenderness swelled inside of her as she thought of

how much Rafe had given her. He'd awakened her in a way she'd never dreamed possible.

They hoarded the cabin's limited supply of canned goods in favor of finding small game.

"Ease up on the string," Rafe instructed as they set a snare, using a bootlace and little else. "That's it."

When she pulled a rabbit from the snare an hour later, she was nearly as proud as she'd been of her first Academy Award.

For dinner, they feasted on rabbit roasted on a spit.

Greedily, she pulled apart the meat with her fingers and wondered what her public would think of America's Sweetheart if they could see her now.

Her humor in the situation faded as she realized she had yet to tell Rafe the truth about herself.

Tell him who you are, her conscience prodded. Once they reached civilization, she couldn't hope to keep it a secret. More important, though, was Rafe's reaction when he learned of her identity.

He'd told her enough about his fiancee to let her understand he wouldn't easily accept deceit. The longer she put it off, the more daunting the prospect became.

Her silence hung between them.

"Rafe."

He turned, dark eyes warm with pleasure as he took in her freshly washed face. "What?"

"I . . . I just wanted you to know that these last days are some of the happiest I can remember."

She'd spoken only the truth to appease the niggling inner voice.

"Same goes."

The different layers of feeling this man generated in her took on a deeper texture. Respect, admiration, tenderness, and love, always love.

They dined on rattlesnake on their final night at the cabin. Was it only a few weeks ago she'd balked at the idea of eating snake?

Apparently Rafe was recalling the same incident.

"Do you remember—"

"Do you remember—"

They laughed, rich and full and long. The sound of it warmed her through and through. She realized they'd reached the stage where they knew what the other was thinking, where words had become superfluous.

She glanced down at herself and grimaced. Never in her life had she more wanted to appear beautiful and appealing. Her discomfort vanished under the warm gaze he rested on her. In her too-big shirt and jeans, she had never felt more like a woman.

Rafe didn't utter a word, only stroked her hand, her cheek. "You are one special lady. Never forget that."

For a moment, she forgot to breathe. She gulped, the sound unnaturally loud in the silence.

She delighted in the strength of his arms, the warmth of his breath as it feathered over her face. She shoved her fingers through his hair. It had grown longer in the last week, to curl over his neck.

Love didn't require comfort. It needed only a chance to grow, to flourish. Right now, she was praying that what she felt for him wasn't one-sided, that he, too, felt the pull of love.

He shaped his palms to her face. "You are so beautiful."

She'd heard the words dozens of times, read them in reviews, seen them in publicity articles. Never had they meant what they did now. If she were beautiful, it was because of the love she knew must shine in her eyes.

Perfect features didn't constitute beauty. Feelings did. Love did. Love made the difference.

Time was running out. She refused to think of that. For now, for this moment, they were together. That was all that mattered.

A stillness settled over her.

He slid his hand beneath her hair, massaging her neck with slow, gentle strokes. "What's up?" he asked when a frown chased across her face.

Joy swirled within her, but it was coupled with despair. "Nothing."

He fitted his hands to her shoulders and turned her to face him. "Nothing doesn't make you look like that."

"What's going to happen?"

"I'm planning on kissing you. Again," he said in that slow drawl that never failed to turn her bones to butter and her brain to mush.

Her smile was slow in coming. "What about when we leave here?"

The teasing light faded from his eyes. "We get you back to LA."

"What about you?"

"I've got a ranch to run."

She'd spent most of her adult life indulging the public's appetite for fantasy. Now she wanted just a bit of that for herself.

Tomorrow would come soon enough. For now, they were together. "It's never been this way."

"Never." He didn't say more.

It was enough to know he felt the same.

This man, this moment, would forever be imprinted on her mind. Her heart.

Chapter Nine

Their last night at the cabin, Rafe held her in his arms, telling her in every way but words how he felt. She knew that he loved her. If only he could get out the words . . .

The following morning, they made the last leg of the trip with trudging steps, and she knew the slow pace was not because of Rafe's injuries. Neither of them wanted this time together to end. Neither wanted to say good-bye.

Or, at least, that was what she told herself.

Within half a day, they spotted the highway. Elation mingled with dread to concoct an uneasy brew in her stomach.

A battered pickup truck stopped. "You folks need a

ride?" The weathered cowboy looked from Star to Rafe, who nodded.

"Thanks."

Rafe helped Star climb inside the truck. Squeezed between him and the burly driver, she concentrated on making herself as small as possible. It wasn't hard. She'd dropped a good ten pounds during the last two weeks.

"You get lost or something?" the rancher asked.

"Or something," Rafe said.

Star couldn't think of anything to add to that and so remained silent. Her churning thoughts occupied all of her concentration, at any rate.

"Rafe, there's something I need—"

The squeal of brakes put a halt to what she'd been about to say. "City limits," the rancher said, gesturing to the sign announcing the township of Quilley, Wyoming, population 10,251. "Can I drop you folks somewhere?"

"You got a diner around here?" Rafe asked. "Somewhere we can get a bite to eat."

"Sure. Polly's Place. Two blocks north. You want I should take you there?"

Rafe turned to Star. "A burger sound good to you?"

It sounded like heaven. And maybe she could find the words to tell him what she should have told him from the beginning.

"Sure."

Their newfound friend delivered them to the diner.

"Polly makes the best burgers this side of the Mississippi."

"Thanks." Rafe stuffed his hand in his pocket, found the wallet that had somehow survived.

"None of that," the man said. "These parts, we look out for each other."

A pink-faced waitress showed them to an old-fashioned booth, complete with red vinyl benches and gray Formica table.

They ordered burgers, shakes, and fries. Star ate without regard to calories, fat grams, sodium content, and all the other things her nutritionist constantly drummed into her. The grease-laden food tasted like glory.

"That's the best food I've ever had," she said after devouring the burger in record time.

Rafe grunted something, swiped his mouth with a napkin, and started in on his second burger. He tipped the ketchup bottle to smear on a small mountain of fries.

Once more, she put off telling him what she needed to say. What difference could another hour, another day make? She glanced up. Was the waitress looking their way?

After their meal, Star bullied Rafe into going to the hospital. She still worried about the possibility of infection from his wounds.

The hospital was small, but well-equipped, the staff efficient and concerned. When it came time to give her name, she did so in a low voice. No one seemed to take notice of her.

"What's wrong?" Rafe asked. "You're fidgeting like a mare about to drop a foal."

She knew he was trying to tease a smile from her, and she did her best to comply.

A nurse arrived to take him to an examination room. At the same moment, a swarm of reporters and photographers appeared.

Star grimaced at the speed with which the media had learned of her identity.

"Ms. Whitney, is it true you were lost in the wilderness for three weeks?"

"What about the cowboy? Are you and he an item?" This last was said with a coy smile and a wink.

Star pushed past the reporters, only to be waylaid by her agent.

"Star, darling, you couldn't have bought better publicity," Brian whispered in her ear.

"Thanks for the concern," she said dryly.

His elation evaporated, to be replaced by a look of sorrow. "You know what I mean."

The entourage of people he felt it necessary to travel with hovered around her.

The studio hairdresser, complete with flowing robes and ponytail, advanced on her. "Star, baby, what did you do to your hair?" He pantomimed a heart attack.

The makeup artist grabbed Star by the chin, turned her head this way and that. "Your skin's a mess. You've got freckles."

She didn't have time for their fussing and brushed them aside. She had to talk with Rafe, make him understand, but he was already walking away.

She hurried to catch up with him. She laid a hand on his arm, felt the tremor of temper in the tensed muscle. "Rafe . . . I can explain."

He rounded on her. "What? That you're some kind of movie star?"

"I wanted to tell you, was going to. Then things got . . . complicated."

"Complicated. Is that what you call it? You must have had a good laugh at the hick cowboy."

"Is that what you think? That I was laughing at you?" She was hotly furious. Even more, she was hurt. Yes, she'd lied to him about her job, but she'd never lied about her feelings.

"Star, sweetheart, we've got to get you—"

She spun to face her agent. "Shut up, Brian." She turned back to Rafe. The cold disinterest in his eyes chilled her all the way to the bone.

"I'll let you get back to your people." The drawl in his voice took on a cold note. "That is what you call them, isn't it?" He stalked away, boot heels clicking on linoleum.

A doctor examined her, pronounced her slightly malnourished but otherwise fit. She rejected Brian's idea of having a team of specialists flown in to look at her.

She stationed herself outside the room where she'd

seen Rafe disappear. She wanted a shower, a flood of steaming water and waves of flowery soap, but was unwilling to leave her post even for a few minutes.

She spent the time avoiding the press and fretting for when she would see Rafe again. Hours passed and still no word from him. She finally swallowed her pride and asked a nurse about him.

The nurse, a kind-eyed woman, informed her Rafe had been moved, at his request, to a local clinic near his ranch. Another question elicited the answer that the transfer had been at his request. The sympathy in her voice made Star feel worse than ever.

Her world collapsed upon itself. She reminded herself she'd see him again. She'd never properly thanked him for taking her with him, for saving her life. It was a flimsy excuse after what they'd shared, but it was all she had.

She took a room at a hotel and indulged herself with the hot shower she'd longed for, clean clothes, and clean sheets. She'd trade them all for a chance to talk with Rafe.

With supreme effort, she focused on practical details, like the car she'd abandoned in the gully. She called a tow truck and made arrangements for it to be towed to a garage.

To her chagrin but hardly to her surprise, reporters continued to pester her. Finally, she agreed to make a statement. The hotel manager arranged for a room.

She stood at a makeshift podium. "I'm here today

because of the courage of the man who rescued me when my car went off the road. I can never repay him for what he did." She took a steadying breath. "To those who have sent cards, made calls, and offered prayers, thank you.

"I won't be answering any questions at this time. I hope you understand." She ignored the clamor of voices and made her escape to the quiet of her room.

After two days had passed, she worked up her courage to call Rafe. She recognized Casey's gruff voice and was told Rafe would be up to receiving visitors at the end of the week.

His use of the word made her wince. Was that what she was? A visitor?

This was a waiting period. She knew if regrets came, they would surface now, while she and Rafe were apart. For some people, absence didn't make the heart grow fonder. For some, absence allowed minds to reconsider, for love to cool, for hearts to forget.

She knew her own heart. She had to wonder if Rafe knew his.

Though Brian wanted to accompany her, she made the trip alone.

The house suited the land she thought as she drove to the Heartsong ranch house in her rented car. Fashioned out of silver-aged cedar and native stone, it melded with its surroundings. Only when she looked closer did she notice the signs of neglect.

The pines towering above the house, nature's sentinels, snagged her attention. Snow-topped mountains, resembling hot fudge sundaes with whipped cream topping, surrounded the homestead. With a backdrop like that, peeling paint and splintered wood hardly mattered.

No flowers softened the ranch yard. She thought of her own carefully tended garden. The citified prettiness of it wouldn't have suited the land. Or the man.

But flowers could survive here, she decided. Wildflowers could withstand the harsh land, and flowers could be transplanted. Look at her. Hadn't she survived a bear attack, a trek over the wilderness?

Her pulse beat dull and thick as she climbed the steps to the front porch, and rapped on the massive oak door.

Rafe let her in. He looked tired, haggard. Dark circles ringed his eyes, as though he hadn't slept in the week since he'd left the hospital. She struggled with the need to put her arms around him and hold him until the flat expression left his eyes. She'd make him remember those days they'd spent together.

"How are you feeling?" she asked carefully, feeling like a fool for uttering such inane words.

"How do you think?" The growl was every bit as ferocious as that of the bear that had mauled him.

So much for polite conversation.

He gestured around. "Take a look. Tell me what you see."

She did as he asked. The room was sparsely furnished, the upholstery threadbare, the braided rug frayed and faded. She took in the well-worn boots placed near the door, the collection of ranching magazines strewn on the coffee table, the family pictures scattered about. "It's a home."

"It used to be a showplace. Back when my mom was alive, the place shone. Dad kept it up as best he could. Then he took sick. The insurance ran out and so did the money."

"What happened?"

"Beef prices went down. Insurance went up. The ranch nearly went under. Still, we were scraping by. Until Gina." His laugh scraped over her like sandpaper. "What she didn't spend on shopping sprees, I spent trying to keep her happy here."

The hope she'd carried in her heart slipped another notch.

She waited. Praying for the words she'd longed to hear. *I love you.* Three simple words, words that had the power to change lives.

Her hands, she noted, were shaking. She clasped them together, as much for support as to hide their trembling.

When it became obvious that he didn't intend on saying anything, she rushed in to fill the silence. "I could help. I have some savings . . ." Too late she realized she'd said exactly the wrong thing.

His expression hardened. "I don't take charity." The word whipped out with the sting of a lash.

Regret vanished to be replaced by fury. She welcomed it. Anger was infinitely preferable. "Is that what you think I'm offering? Charity?" She was surprised she didn't choke on the word.

Her hands made a slicing motion. "You were willing to die rather than admit you needed help out there. Just how far will you go to hold on to your precious pride?"

She struggled to control the emotions seething inside her. She dug her nails into her palms and took short, shallow breaths. Her anger died as suddenly as it erupted when she looked at him. The pain she saw in his eyes nearly broke her. Why couldn't he accept that she loved him? Would always love him.

"You don't understand." The words were uttered in such a low voice she had to strain to catch them.

"Don't I?" The question hung between them, a challenge that couldn't be ignored. "Pride is your enemy. It always has been."

How did she know? It was his dark secret, his pride. Pride in his refusal to sell the ranch. Pride in his refusal to take the easy way out. Pride in himself.

"I know because I face the same enemy," she said, surprising him enough to have his eyes flicking to hers. "Every day. Every hour. You don't think I battled pride? Pride in what I've achieved, what I've done with my life. The poor Latina girl from the wrong side of the tracks becomes a star. Give me some credit. Of course I'm proud. So proud that sometimes I forget where I've come from. I can't ever afford to do that."

"You belong to a different world," he said. "A world

so far removed from mine the difference could be measured in light years rather than miles."

"I belong here. With you."

"What about your work? You can't tell me it doesn't matter."

"Of course it matters. Just as your work matters to you. But it doesn't have to keep us apart." She'd made her mark and if she never did another movie, she wouldn't feel cheated. The only person who could cheat her was Rafe.

They could make it work. If only he was willing to take a chance. On them.

The pain was so intense she swore she felt her heart stop beating. When it started up again, she was sure he must hear it, so fiercely did it pound in her chest. He was telling her good-bye. She blinked away the mist in her eyes and leveled her breathing.

Stupid man. All he thought of were salaries—his and hers. Didn't he know that those were so unimportant as to not be worth mentioning at all? If it was a choice between him and her career, there was no choice.

"I'm good enough to walk through the desert with you, but not good enough to love. Is that it?" Her eyes began to tear and she blanked them dry.

He didn't flinch, didn't give any sign that her words reached him, that they mattered, that she mattered. "I didn't want it to end this way."

A door slammed somewhere. She thought the sound

she heard was the crack of her own heart. Once more she was that little girl in her grandmother's house, wanting desperately to be loved.

She felt the light die from her eyes, and the hope from her heart. Still, she tried again. "If it made a difference, I'd give up acting. But it doesn't, does it? You love me, but you're too much of a coward to admit it." She pushed the words out as though shoving boulders off her chest.

"You're off base. You've caused me nothing but trouble from the moment we met. I knew it with the first whiff of your fancy perfume."

She bit her lip, hoping to focus on that rather than the words that carved pieces off her heart. "You're so afraid to admit you might have feelings that you'd do anything to avoid them. Including sending me away."

"You're way off the mark."

His anger fueled her determination to convince him otherwise. "Am I? Everything that happens, happens for a purpose. Why is it so hard to believe there was a special reason that we met?"

"You're talking in riddles."

"Maybe. And maybe we were meant to be brought together."

"You don't belong here."

Pain twisted around her heart like barbs. She drew a breath, shuddered it out. She shoved it into a neat little box and tucked it away somewhere deep inside. If she gave in to it, she wouldn't be able to function through the next few minutes, let alone the days and weeks to follow.

"I belong wherever you are." Her eyes, luminous with unshed tears, didn't waver from his. "I love you, Rafe Mackenzie. Nothing's going to change that. Not even you."

Her words sucked the breath straight from his lungs. He stared at her, afraid to believe what she said, afraid not to.

Reason . . . and fear . . . won out. "Look, princess, we knew the score when we started. You go back to your life and I stay here." His stomach might be twisted in greasy knots of tension, but his voice was as flat as the prairie.

Heck, he was giving the performance of his life. He deserved one of those awards they made such a fuss about in Hollywood.

The pain in her eyes lashed his heart with stinging stripes. He steeled himself against it, against her. Better to hurt her now than watch her love turn to hate. Or, worse, pity.

It was only a matter of time before the mist of romance cleared from her eyes and she realized what he already had: that he could never fit into her world and he wouldn't ask her to fit into his.

"That's it?" She couldn't keep the pleading from her voice. "What am I supposed to do? Say good-bye and forget you, forget everything that happened?"

"Nothing happened." He shrugged with what he

hoped was convincing casualness. Because it was tearing the heart from him, he hardened his voice. "We
shared some good times. That's all."

"You don't mean it."

"It's over. You have a life out there." He gestured
widely. "Mine's here."

"Tell me you don't want me and I'll leave."

He shoved his hands inside his pockets, careful to
keep his face expressionless. It took every ounce of
willpower he had to say what he had to. "I don't want
you." Pain layered the words, but she didn't seem to
notice.

She wasn't sure she could speak, that the words she
wanted, needed to say, would push through her raw
throat. "You love me. And you'll wonder what we
might have had, what we might have shared, if not for
your cowardice." She used the back of her hand to wipe
her eyes dry.

Her lashes, wet and spiky, shuttered her eyes before
she looked up at him again. "Good-bye, Rafe." She
turned and walked away, head high, slim back poker-
straight.

She moved with such fluid grace, he thought, when
she'd been fighting off the grizzly, and now. He hadn't
been able to forget the gallant courage she'd showed
then, or anything else about her.

"Wait." He reached for the chain around his neck,
and fumbled. "Here. It's yours."

She stared at the medallion. "I can't take it. Your father gave it to you."

"I want you to have it. You've earned it. It'll remind you of where you've been. Maybe it'll help you figure out where you're going."

She pressed it between her hands, bit down on the despair that pinched her heart at the same time. The hard metal edges bit into her palms, but the pain barely registered. "I don't have any idea where I'm going." She'd never said anything truer.

"You will when you get there." He cupped her face between his palms. "Good-bye, my Estrella. *Via con dios.*"

She marched past him, out the door, careful with every step not to falter or look back. Her legs felt like glass, the fragile kind that could be shattered with a careless swipe of the hand.

The rest of her was numb. Dead.

Rafe watched as she walked away. He thought of the pain he'd brought to her eyes and knew it would haunt him for all of his days.

Casey should have known when to leave bad enough alone, but he took one look at Rafe and scowled. "You look like something the coyotes ate and then spit out. Should have stayed at the hospital longer."

"They can't fix what's wrong with me." The concern in his old friend's face only added to Rafe's misery. "Don't you have some fence to mend?"

Rafe winced as a shaft of guilt lanced through him. He had no call to speak to Casey that way. Casey had been trying only to help, and Rafe had thrown it back in his face. Casey had had the back luck of being a handy target.

"Never knew you to be a coward. Looks like I was wrong." After giving Rafe a long look that held as much pity as it did censure, Casey took himself off.

Coward. A voice whispered the taunt in his ear throughout the rest of the day. He didn't ignore it, he accepted it. And knew he was going to have to learn how to live with it.

Barbed wire.

He hated the stuff. Years of working with it hadn't changed that. If he hadn't spent so much time mooning over Star, he'd have finished the job yesterday.

Deer foraged closer to town, looking for food. They knocked the fences down faster than he and his men could repair them. Just what he needed. He stood in the unrelenting wind and smelled hints of winter. The days had grown shorter, the nights longer with the dark pulling farther and farther over the light. The damp of autumn clung to the ground.

If he didn't get the fence repaired soon, the cattle would discover the hole in it and wander away. Dumb animals didn't know enough to stay put.

But his mind wasn't on repairing fences. It wasn't on

the profit-and-loss statements that put fear in any rancher's heart. It was remembering the scent that was Star's alone, the feel of her as she wrapped her arms around him, the softness of her mouth when he moved his lips over hers.

It was only about the hundredth time in the last hour that memories of her had interfered with his concentration.

In the last week, he'd done some digging and read everything he could find about her. She'd told the truth about her beginnings, the struggle to get where she was. It took guts to rise above that. But to use it, instead of being used by it, that took more.

It took valor.

He wasn't surprised. Hadn't she shown that same valor when she'd attacked a bear with only a puny stick? And what of her struggle to get both of them to safety? Everything about her showed courage, mettle, and determination.

What had made him think he was getting over her? He was as much in love with her as ever. He unwound a coil of wire and tried to obliterate the picture of Star's face that had stuck in his mind.

His efforts were wasted, as he'd known they would be. She'd worked her way into his mind, and his heart, as no one had before.

He lifted his gaze to the masterpiece of color only nature could produce. The sky was the color of strained peaches and laced with clouds, the air so suddenly sweet that he felt intoxicated by it. How had he managed to ignore the beauty that surrounded him?

Lately, he'd deliberately ignored the magnificence of his mountain home, preferring to nurse his pain. His brooding had netted him a case of self-pity that would have disgraced even a Hollywood neurotic.

Once more, his thoughts turned to Star. She had appreciated nature's splendor, delighting in all of its colors and moods. He clamped down on the direction his reflections had taken and hit the staple off center. It flew out of his gloved fingers. The coiled wire he'd been trying to tighten slipped free and lashed out at him.

Snapping his head back, he managed to avoid the worst of it, but not before one of the barbs caught him across the jaw. He swiped at his face with the back of his hand, not surprised when his glove came away bloody.

He couldn't spare the time to take care of it now. If he didn't get this section of fence mended before the first snow came, he'd have to wait until next spring before the ground dried out. Fencing and mud didn't mix. The shaky line between autumn and winter didn't last long.

When snow came, they'd drive the cattle down to the low meadow. An early blizzard could wipe out a herd grazing in the high country. But there was time yet.

He had learned to interpret nature's signs. A lifetime of ranch work had taught him how to feel the changes in the weather. It was a good life. He couldn't imagine doing anything else.

Just a couple more to go. Resolutely, he picked up the wire and finished the post before moving on to the next one.

He'd crammed more and more into each day, determined to crowd out thoughts of Star. One good thing about a ranch the size of his was that the work was never finished. He'd kept a tight hold on the reins of running it these last weeks, taking over what belonged to Casey.

It was only a matter of time before Casey called him on it. That he chose today when Rafe's temper was already on a short fuse was just plain bad luck. For both of them.

"You want to hold the post or work the wire?" Rafe asked when Casey showed up, a scowl on his lips and trouble in his eyes.

Pride wouldn't let Casey take the easier job, and he picked up the coil of wire. Rafe knew better than to protest. You sweat beside a man day after day, year after year, and you come to know him.

He and Casey had been working alongside each other for more than twenty years. Arthritis may have slowed Casey down, but he fought through it, insisting on keeping to a schedule that would have killed many a younger man.

Rafe understood pride. He had his own share of it and wouldn't take it from the man who had been both friend and mentor for more than two decades.

They worked silently, falling into a rhythm honed to smooth perfection over the years. Rafe didn't bother asking what Casey wanted. Casey wasn't one to be rushed. He'd tell Rafe in his own way, his own time.

"Can't a man find a few minutes of peace around here?" Rafe muttered, unable to stand another minute of his foreman's tight-lipped silence. His fingers curled around the hammer until his fist ran white across the knuckles.

"Nope." Casey lowered the coil of wire to the ground and huffed out a breath, the only concession he'd make to the backbreaking work. He planted his hands on his scrawny hips and glared at Rafe. "Your manners are as rusty as a dead horse's shoe."

Rafe glared back.

"You've been downright ornery ever since you sent the pretty lady away. Like a bear with its head caught in a beehive." Casey had used the same tone when Rafe had been ten and throwing a tantrum when his father wouldn't let him ride a just-broke stallion.

Rafe winced. "Thanks for the observation. Anything else you wanted to say?"

"What I want doesn't matter. It's what you want. You're plumb crazy." Casey squinted, as though studying something particularly loathsome. "Hadn't noticed it before, but it stands out at close quarters." His words cut through Rafe's self-pity. "That little gal loves you."

"I thought you didn't like her."

"Didn't. That don't mean I can't change my mind

and 'fess up when I've been wrong. She took to trail life like a hog to slop. Had grit to spare."

Rafe felt a grin tug at his lips at Star's likely reaction to the metaphor.

"That gal's got spine."

High praise indeed from Casey.

"From the way you tell it, she saved your butt. You want her," he said when Rafe remained stubbornly silent. "So you send her away. Not smart. Never took you for a fool, boy. Looks like I was wrong."

Rafe saw the red haze at the edges of his vision, a sure sign temper was gaining the upper hand and he was on the verge of doing something stupid. He took a deliberate breath. Another.

Trust Casey to cut to the heart of the matter. No mincing words for him. Rafe considered firing the older man and rejected it. He'd fired Casey at least twenty times over the years, and each time Casey had ignored him.

Rafe was honest enough to admit he couldn't manage without his old friend. He was pigheaded enough to want to try.

"You're a gossipy old woman. Why don't you mind your own business?" he asked, but the words were said without rancor.

"When you stop acting like a prize fool," came the no-nonsense reply.

Rafe pretended not to have heard.

"Sometimes in this world, the truth ain't hardly a

kindness. Then, others, it's the best friend a man's got. That's why I'm telling you. Go and get your lady. You aren't worth buzzard spit the way you are."

Rafe's lips curved up in a reluctant grin. Casey had torn strips off his hide on a regular basis when Rafe had been growing up. No one chewed him out better. Except Star. The thought caused his smile to slip a notch.

"It wouldn't have worked." If he said the words often enough, he might begin to believe them. His hands curled into fists. She belonged in a flower garden, not the untamed land he called home.

Casey's jaw slid to the side as though he didn't believe a word Rafe was feeding him. "You're stuck on her. I know it, and so do you. Your father didn't raise a fool. Neither did I."

Rafe glared at his friend and bit back words he knew would hang ugly between them.

Casey suffered the glare with equanimity.

Rafe's temper died as quickly as it had erupted, the fire in his eyes dwindling to a simmer. He unclenched his hands, forced himself to relax. "Sorry."

"You always did have a short fuse, boy."

Boy. Rafe hadn't been a boy in twenty years, but old habits died hard. Casey was the only one who called him that, the only one who dared call him that.

"I always could count on you to cheer me up."

"If you don't watch it, you're gonna end up old and alone. Like me."

Rafe stared. That was the first time he'd heard Casey use the word *old*, much less complain about being alone. How had he missed his friend's dissatisfaction?

"If a woman ever looked at me the way that little filly looked at you, I'd fall down on my knees and promise her I'd love her forever."

Rafe started to say something, thought better about it.

"Don't go getting all sloppy about it," Casey warned, rumpled face reddening. "I made my bed a long time ago. Nobody's fault." He fixed Rafe with a fierce stare. "Just make sure you know what you're doing. Pride's all well and good, but it won't ease a lonely heart."

They finished the job, Rafe mulling over what Casey had said. After they loaded up the truck and returned to the homestead, he saddled Bear, knowing he needed the freedom of a fast gallop over the land.

"Casey." The older man stopped, turned. "Thanks."

"Go ride off your mean, then put that horse up the way you've been taught," Casey said gruffly. He slapped the reins against Rafe's thigh.

They both knew Rafe didn't need the reminder. It was Casey's way of saying what he couldn't put into words.

With that, the roughest edge of Rafe's anger smoothed. Riding was the best cure he knew to cut through the tangle of his thoughts and ease the ache in his heart. This was the land of his childhood. He knew every mountain, every valley, every ridge.

Bear took the rough ground without a hitch.

Rafe hadn't realized how much he needed the feel of the wind against his face, the pounding of hooves beneath him until he and Bear had covered several miles. He needed space, away from everyone and everything.

What's more, he needed time to think. Not about Star, he assured himself. There was nothing to think about there. That was settled. Over.

He drew up on the reins and slowed Bear to a trot. The big gelding snorted his displeasure at the slower speed.

"Easy," Rafe said in a low voice.

When he found himself at the edge of a canyon, staring down at the emptiness below, he stopped, stared. The place was as cold and empty as the black hole of his heart. The wind cut through the canyon with the bite of winter in its teeth.

He felt his aloneness all the way to the core. Not loneliness. He didn't yearn for company. He was alone in the truest sense of the word.

Because of pride.

There was that word again, a word he'd fought to rid himself of. But it crept back, insidiously, insistently, waiting to trip him up.

He wanted to dismiss Casey's words as the meanderings of an old man. The truth was Casey was as sharp as ever. What's more, he wasn't one to talk just to hear the sound of his own voice. That he cared enough to say something was proof in itself that the listener had better sit up and take notice.

Sure, Star might think the idea of playing rancher's wife sounded fun. But what about when the temperature dropped to ten below zero and the calves had to be fed? How would she feel when he was gone from sunup to midnight and came home so bone tired that he could barely stand, much less take her out dancing? And what of the crueler parts of ranching—the branding, the castrating, the putting down of animals too sick to save?

How could he expect Star to cope with that kind of life? In his reading on her, he discovered that not only was she an actress, but a bona-fide star. The tabloids liked to sprinkle her name through their pages.

With every word he read, his spirits plummeted further. If he'd had any doubts before about Star's ability to adapt to ranch life, they disappeared. A lot of women born and bred to the life couldn't handle the hardships of it. He'd seen it more than once.

Gina, a city girl like Star, hadn't been able to bear the isolation, the bitter cold of winter, the unceasing wind.

He couldn't give Star the kind of life she was accustomed to, and living off his wife's money didn't sit well with him. Star didn't understand. A man took care of his woman. He didn't lean on anyone, especially those he'd sworn to protect, to care for. A sigh leaked out of his lungs.

He couldn't do it. Wouldn't do it. A man had his pride. The argument sounded hollow, even to his own ears. Pride was a lonely companion, as Casey had reminded him.

He had to be fair to Star, no matter what the cost to him. Honesty forced him to admit, if only to himself, that it wasn't Star he was looking out for.

It was himself.

To have Star look at him one day as nothing more than a promise she must keep would destroy him. He knew that as surely as he knew his own name. He couldn't chance it. Better a half life without her, than to risk losing his soul when she left.

And what of her career? She was at the top and destined to remain so for years to come. He couldn't, wouldn't, ask her to give that up. He'd heard of marriages where husband and wife lived in different states, meeting on weekends. He wanted more than that. So much more.

He knew she said she didn't mind the isolation, the lack of money, the unending work. But what about six months from now, a year? Or two? And what of children? A career in Hollywood and children didn't make a good combination.

The questions swarmed around inside his head, tormenting, taunting, until he could no longer think. He forced them from his mind. He had made the right choice, the logical, intelligent choice. The only choice.

But if it were so logical, so intelligent, why did his

heart feel as if it had been torn in half? Thanks to him, she was gone, so why couldn't he stuff all those unwanted feelings back where they belonged? Why did the past month seem so bleak? And the future even bleaker?

He concentrated on the sun dropping behind the gray-green mountains. The rosy sky deepened with every minute he stood there. It helped ease the chill around his heart.

An impatient whicker from Bear reminded him they'd remained there too long. "You're right, boy," Rafe murmured. "Enough daydreaming."

They made the trip home with none of the earlier urgency. At the ridge overlooking the homestead, he lifted his head and gazed below—the corrals, the out-buildings, the paddocks, and farther to where the land rolled forth to meet the sky. The endless expanse of land and sky was balm to his wounded soul.

This last stretch, the worn path to the homestead, never failed to reach out to him, to stroke away the exhaustion. Through drought and land-grabbing, fire and flood, the Heartsong had stood and withstood.

For more than a hundred years, it had remained in Mackenzie hands. It had nourished them, nurtured them, birthed them, and, when the time came, buried them.

Now it was his.

Rafe led Bear into the stable and began the rubdown routine he'd been taught to do nearly as soon as he'd learned to walk. He couldn't remember a time when he hadn't been riding or working the land.

Cold and hungry, he didn't have the energy or inclination to sort through his emotions. He wanted a hot shower, clean clothes, and a warm meal, in that order. He tried not to think of Star.

Of course, he thought of her.

His cry cut through the night, shattering its stillness. The lady made it difficult to forget her. He ached for her, a physical pain that reached down and squeezed his heart until it felt wrung dry of all feeling.

Loneliness wasn't something that had bothered him in the past, but he hadn't known how alone he truly was until Star.

She had shown him his heart.

Chapter Ten

W hen her agent messengered a script to her, with a note that it might be "just what you've been looking for," Star pulled herself out of her misery long enough that she could actually use her brain.

After clucking and fussing over her absence and then playing her up as some kind of real-life heroine, Brian had worked to get back into her good graces, up to and including beating the bushes for the kind of part for which she was looking.

The script was a peace offering. Brian was too good an agent, and, more, too good a friend, for her to hold a grudge for long. She owed it to him, and to herself, to shake off the depression she'd wallowed in for the last month.

After a quick read, she felt the first stirring of

excitement she'd experienced in weeks. The script was rough, but it had grit. What's more, it would test her, make her dig deep inside herself for the talent to make it shine. She settled back, preparing to read it again, this time with an eye to what she could bring to it.

There was substance in it she thought three hours later. Substance and merit. The heroine was no naive ingenue, untried and untested, but a woman with backbone and pluck.

Like her.

The words resounded through her with a force that took her breath away.

She could do it. She *was* this woman. Hadn't she fought off a bear with nothing more than a branch and reckless courage, saving the life of the man she loved? Hadn't she treated Rafe's wounds with only herbs and boiling water? Hadn't she struggled through an unknown land, practically carrying him most of the way?

And hadn't she, despite all odds, fallen in love?

She was a strong woman who was only now discovering just how strong she truly was. Before Rafe, she'd still been that naive girl, unaware of the ordeals she would face on the trail, and in life. She'd emerged a woman, tested by both nature and man, and she'd survived. She had proved herself.

Perhaps Brian had been right in refusing to allow her to try tougher roles before now. He'd seen something in her since her return that had convinced him that she could handle a more demanding part.

She set the script down and knew it was everything she'd hoped for. Her professional life was soaring. She was in the enviable position of being able to pick and choose, to take on only projects that interested her. Now she had a story line that boasted both a great plot and wonderful characters.

Only one thing upset the equation. A hard-headed man with too much pride and not enough sense. Given a choice, she'd chuck everything and return to Wyoming, to the man she loved.

She'd been feeling fine, almost normal, until the memory of Rafe had come out of nowhere to ambush her.

Would it always be this way?

She had met other men who were equally handsome, equally powerful, equally strong. Yet none were as compelling as one battered cowboy in worn jeans and scuffed boots.

A date with her co-star last night, arranged by her publicist, had left her cold. Normally she made it a policy not to get involved with people in the industry. Even so, she wondered why Jake Marsh failed to interest her.

Certainly, he was attractive, with his blond hair and perfectly sculpted body. He'd been charming, witty, and flatteringly attentive. She'd felt nothing, except ill-concealed boredom.

Therein lay the problem. Every man suffered by comparison to Rafe. All came up wanting.

Tinseltown had a surfeit of good-looking men. They came in all ages, all sizes, all intellects. None of them piqued her interest. None of them caused her heart to flutter and her insides to turn to mush. None of them made her want to abandon the goals she'd set for herself a lifetime ago.

Good going, girl. You managed to fall in love with a cowboy who could have stepped right out of the 19th century. She, who had played the heroine in westerns, had found an honest-to-goodness hero. The only trouble was, he refused to recognize that they could ride off into the sunset together.

Her whole life had been a search to discover what was wrong with her. With Rafe, she'd felt cherished. Whole. There was no longer the burning need to find the missing part, the part that would make her worthy of loving.

How ironic that the one man who made her feel that way was the same one who had rejected her. She knew he loved her. She couldn't have mistaken his feelings, but she also knew he was fighting himself.

He didn't want her, didn't want any chance of a future together. He preferred his solitude and his pride.

Was she a fool for continuing to care? Time and distance should have dimmed the feelings she carried for him, yet her love hadn't faded. If anything, it had grown.

She missed his wry sense of humor, his sharp insights, even his temper. If she allowed herself to think, she could remember the feel of his lips, the touch of his hands.

It was her gift and her curse to know her heart so well, for there would be no other man after Rafe. She might seek companionship, but her heart would remain true. Not out of choice, she admitted, but out of pain.

What caprice of fate had brought her to this point? Who could say why she'd chosen the route that had put her in Rafe's path? Why had the rabbit chosen to dart in front of her at that particular spot?

Undoubtedly, there had been logical reasons for each of the choices that had taken her closer to where she was today. But a woman in love didn't want logic.

So why was she analyzing every step that had brought Rafe into her life? The memory of their last words to each other smeared her heart with misery. Tempted to wallow in it, she shook away the worst of it.

Hunger drove her from her self-imposed isolation. She drove to her favorite restaurant and ordered a steak and salad. Rather than enjoy it, she remembered eating rattlesnake at a campfire. There was no smell of woodsmoke in the trendy restaurant, no tall stories or off-key singing. She missed them desperately.

She turned her head as the sound of laughter drifted her way. The couple sitting knee to knee in a far booth was oblivious to everyone but each other. She had no idea of who they were, but it was their pleasure in each other that held her attention. They gave off sparks, small, delighted sounds of a man and a woman who had just discovered they love each other.

The sight stirred her envy. And her heart.

The slightest touch turned up the love that shimmered between them. She could see it in their flushed faces, a glow that transcended even the muted lighting of the restaurant. It was obvious that no one in the world existed but them.

When she returned home, the pristine state of her condo depressed her. No welcoming smells of cooking greeted her, no aftershave or distinctive musk to contrast with the potpourri she set out. Only the scent of a woman alone.

Alone and lonely.

Maybe she had been playing games after all. She, who had always prided herself on her honesty, had lied. First to Rafe. And then to herself. She'd spun dreams, even while denying doing so, and had had the bad judgment to include Rafe in them.

She had no one to blame but herself.

She let her gaze move over the room, noting the small touches she'd added—a faded quilt from a flea market, her collection of thimbles, the vintage movie posters—failed to bring her comfort. She'd surrounded herself with things she loved, some priceless, some frankly junk.

She'd built this world, she thought, this wedge of serenity surrounded by the noise and energy and confusion of the city. She needed this sanctuary. With its quiet and peace, she could ease away from the pressure and demands of her career.

Twilight, with its softening air, dwindled into evening, evening into the empty hours of the night. She barely repressed a shudder. Nights held their own special kind of misery, a loneliness so acute that it was a palpable thing.

She strolled out to the deck. Stars winked, the moon played hide and seek behind a cloud. The ocean stretched beyond, a deeper black than the sky.

She found no pleasure in the view as she once had. Perhaps if she was sharing it with someone, she might recapture the sense of wonder she'd once felt upon seeing the miles of uninterrupted water.

A breeze stirred. She listened, waiting.

For what?

The lowing of cattle. The whisper of the desert wind. The high country, with air so sharp and crisp that it burned the lungs. The low tones of men talking after a long day. The crackle and snap of dying embers from the campfire.

Her thoughts took her full circle. Back to Rafe. She ached for the man she would never have. She would give anything to have him hold her again, just hold her in that way that made everything inside her yearn and long.

The movie deal came together with a speed that left her in awe. With some fine-tuning, the script was even better than she dared hope. The director seemed pleased with her interpretation of the role, and she felt a rapport with him that promised good things for the future.

She touched the medallion she wore. She hadn't removed it since Rafe had given it to her.

The director frowned. "Lose the jewelry."

"It stays."

He looked like he wanted to argue, then shrugged. "Have it your way. We'll work it into the script. Somehow."

The role was all she'd hoped for. It gave her a chance to show her mettle. Without the weeks with Rafe, she doubted she'd be able to bring all that she did to the part. As it was, she was drawing deep within herself and knew she was giving the best performance of her life.

"You've changed," the director said abruptly.

"Have I?"

"It's in the way you move, the way you hold yourself." He shook his head. "There's more. I can't put my finger on it, but I like it."

At one time, his words would have elated her. Though she appreciated the sentiment, she knew she didn't have to look outside herself for validation. Not any longer.

She went through the scene again, noting the blocking, the stage directions, filing them away for later.

"Okay, people," the assistant director said. "Primp and crimp time."

The predictable moans followed.

Despite her excitement over the project, Star would have preferred to skip the more tedious aspects of her profession, like the two hours she spent while a half dozen people fussed over her hair and face.

She headed to her dressing room where she gave the pots of creams and colors designed to make her beautiful a disgusted glance. They were evidences of the world that kept her apart from Rafe. She'd take twelve hours on location anytime over being blushed and powdered, blown and dried.

Jackie, the makeup artist, hissed out a breath. "Jeez, Whitney. You've got shadows around your eyes dark enough to hide in. And I can count the circles."

Star actually felt her mouth arrange itself in a sulk, before her sense of humor kicked in. She made a face at her reflection in the mirror. "Thanks. Remind me to have you write my press releases."

Jackie ignored that. "My job is to make you look good. So assume the position and let me do my thing."

Star leaned back. In truth, it felt good. The gentle massage of face and neck, the cool soothing of rich cream slathered on her skin. She didn't even mind— too much—the application of the too-heavy makeup, remembering that pores filled with gunk for hours at a time were the price she paid to have a flawless complexion on screen.

Jackie kept up a running commentary of shop talk. Who got the shaft from the producers. Who was hot. Who was not.

Star listened, grateful she wasn't expected to add anything.

She opened her eyes and blinked. Jackie had indeed worked a miracle. Gone were the shadows, the faint bruising around her eyes. Her skin shimmered and her eyes glowed under the application of concealer and shadow.

The staff of people paid to primp and style her disappeared, and she was allowed a much welcome fifteen minutes alone before she was due on the set.

The discordant music coming from a radio battered her eardrums, diminishing only slightly when she closed the door to her dressing room. She didn't turn on her own radio in defense, as she once might have, preferring the relative quiet. Funny how the bluster of the wind blowing over the prairie or the gentle lowing of cattle at night meshed with your mind and soothed your soul, while man-made sounds pummeled and disturbed.

Even the promise of a new direction in her career failed to excite her as it might once have. She was pining for the high country, a place that went bright and beautiful with the setting of the sun, where columbine bloomed in the stingy shade, where the air was so clean you could taste it, and the landscape a child's paintbox of colors.

More, she was pining for the man.

She took another look in the mirror. Her face wasn't something she thought about often, even considered. Her so-called beauty hadn't been an asset when it came to Rafe.

He didn't want her. He'd made that clear the last time

they'd seen each other. That knowledge still had the power to shake her down to the core, to her heart.

Rafe had rejected her love. More important, he had rejected her. The searing pain of it still had the power to bring her to her knees. How had she thought she was over him? Self-delusion, she thought with wry self-deprecation. Men like Rafe Mackenzie had that effect on women.

He'd look good on film, she thought absently. His rugged good looks would translate well on to the big screen. The idea nearly made her smile. Rafe had no use for movies or those who made them. He had no use for her.

She didn't mind the sixteen-hour days. In fact, she welcomed them. They left her exhausted, too weary to torment herself with memories. When she crawled into bed at night, she was asleep within minutes.

The script was even better than she dared hope, the director creative and demanding, the cast professional and dedicated. It was a dream come true.

So why wasn't she happy?

Okay, she had lost the one man she would ever love. That didn't mean she had to curl up in a corner and feel sorry for herself. She'd spent enough time doing that.

Brooding and looking inward wouldn't bring the happiness she sought. With that in mind, she started looking outward. And determined that she could make a difference.

A little research netted the information that a community theater group was floundering due to poor management and a lack of funds.

With help from her accountant, she arranged an anonymous infusion of cash into the group's treasury. That was the easy part.

Now came the time for her to put herself out for someone else. She squeezed two hours out of a day that had no hours to spare and made her way to the small theater, located in the seamier part of the city.

Ridiculously nervous, she approached the man who looked like he might be in charge. "Uh . . . I wondered if I could volunteer."

"Sure," he said absently. "We always need help in painting scenery. If you sew—" He looked up, registered who she was, and dropped his clipboard.

They both bent to pick it up at the same time and knocked heads. She rubbed her forehead, decided she wasn't in any danger of passing out.

Careful of each other, they both stood.

"Star Whitney. Ms. Whitney. I didn't know . . . that is, I didn't know it was you."

Taking pity on him, she smiled. "Of course you didn't. And I meant what I said. I'd like to help."

She spent the next hour listening to his vision of *Our Town*, the classic that every small theater group felt compelled to stage at least once.

"You have a good grasp of the play. Maybe if you switched your emphasis to . . ."

Happily, they discussed a new direction. With her promise to come by the following day, she left, but not before she complimented the awe-struck cast on their work.

She kept her promise, and more. She raided the wardrobe closet at the studio and came away with an armload of costumes that would bring a professional touch to the production.

"I don't know how to thank you," the director said after she finished giving an impromptu acting lesson to the young heroine of the piece.

"I had something in mind." And she proceeded to tell him about the group home for autistic children.

"I'd like to bring them to a special performance. Maybe a matinee. If you can arrange it."

"We'll do that and more. We'll donate the first night's profits to the home. In your name."

"No. I mean, that's great if you can help the children, but not in my name. Please."

Seeing the distress in her eyes, the director nodded. "We'll do it your way."

Well pleased with the both of them, she held out her hand. "Thank you."

"No, Ms. Whitney—Star," he amended with a smile. "Thank you."

She had another stop before she returned home. The city pound.

Intending to bring home a cuddly kitten, she found

her interest snagged by a yellow tom, missing a back leg. Despite that, or maybe because of it, he moved with a dignity that would do a lion proud.

"You don't want that one," a volunteer said. "He's on the list to be disposed of come the end of the week. He's got a mean streak as long as his tail."

In unison, they looked at the bushy tail, easily as thick as her wrist.

That decided it. She brought home the yellow tom, named him Bailey, and decided they might just rescue each other.

Chapter Eleven

Rafe had managed to alienate most of the ranch hands. Casey pointedly avoided him after Rafe got into a stupid argument with his foreman about where to winter the main herd. He seemed to be on everyone's list lately.

He couldn't remember the last time he'd been so weary and so off his stride. He figured the biggest favor he could do the world was steer clear of everyone and hole up in his office.

A chinook wind warmed the day. He opened the window, wanting to let some sunshine into his life. Not even the perfect autumn day could drive away the darkness inside him, though. He carried it with him. A man couldn't escape himself, no matter how hard he ran.

His sense of doom thickened. For what seemed the

thousandth time, he told himself it was for the best. A woman like Star would soon grow bored with nothing but cattle and ranch hands for company. He had nothing to offer but a truckload of debts and a love of the land.

Other parts of the operation were necessary; the windmills, the horse boarding for neighbors. He used them, juggled them, worked them. But they didn't own his heart.

The land did.

The roundup had been successful. The Heartsong Ranch would show a profit for the first time in three years, but he still had a drawer full of bills to pay off. He'd plow whatever money was left back into the land. Too little money and too little time. A rancher's lament.

Scanning the latest printout of the ranch's profit and loss statement, he found his mind wandering. What was Star doing?

Why did he find himself thinking of her at odd moments? It didn't matter what he was doing—putting up a fence, tending a sick calf, or working on end-of-the month reports—his mind conjured up pictures of her.

The lady had invaded his thoughts to the point that he couldn't even trust himself shaving for fear of cutting his face to pieces.

For a few minutes, he indulged in a fantasy of Star and him building a future together. The fantasy dissolved as reality hit him. What did he know about commitment? Or permanency? Or loving and cherishing a woman?

His track record in that department was lousy.

He wasn't the right man for her. Someday, she'd understand that and appreciate the fact that he'd had the good sense to get out of her life before he destroyed the love she'd offered him. She'd get over him eventually and find someone who'd love her as she deserved to be loved.

A mirthless smile tightened his lips.

She'd find someone else. Someone who could give her everything she deserved. Someone who wasn't scarred by the past, someone who knew how to love. She'd was too lovely, too giving to stay alone for long.

If he was any kind of a man, he'd be happy for her when it happened. And he would be, he promised himself fiercely. Even if it killed him.

Work was the best antidote, and he threw himself into it with a vengeance. That served to remind him what he had to offer a woman: Impossible hours, bitter cold in the winters and too short summers, and work enough to break a man if he let it. Not much to recommend it, nothing except that it was all he'd ever known, all he'd ever wanted.

What kind of woman would want to share it? The job of a rancher's wife was no less demanding. Feeding twenty-plus hands during roundup, tending the minor cuts and injuries that came with ranch life, pulling calves in the middle of the night, living with a man too tired to do more than yank off his boots and fall into bed at night. Yeah, it was a picnic, all right. A real picnic.

It was his life, though, and he loved it with a passion as big as the land itself.

The arguments fell flat as he acknowledged that life without Star was no life at all.

He'd lived in the house for all of his life. In the family cemetery, his mother and father were buried. After Gina had left, the place was quiet, but not lonely.

All it had taken was a couple of weeks with Star and his life seemed empty. Without her, a vital part of him was missing. How could he go back to his self-imposed solitude after sharing so much with her?

It was a depressing picture, all the more so because he'd realized how barren his life had been before she had barged her way into it, how barren the future looked.

He thought of Gina, waiting for the familiar guilt to ram him in the gut. He tensed for the expected blow. Nothing. Hardly daring to believe that it was gone, he probed the far corners of his heart, much as he would a toothache, unable to leave it alone. There was no pain left, only a regret for what might have been.

A warm, heavy feeling filled him. The feeling had a name. Forgiveness. Star had given him that. She'd taught him that his guilt was a kind of selfishness, believing he could control the fate of others. Star with her shining honesty and loving heart. Star with her quiet strength and unyielding courage. Star, the woman he'd sent away.

It had been over a month since he'd sent her away, a month during which he'd been dying a little more each day. That the wound was self-inflicted only added to his misery. And his disgust with himself.

He was still fighting his old demon, pride, and acting like a coyote with its leg caught in a steel trap. He could gnaw it off or just wait to die. Either way, he lost.

Pride didn't seem very important beside the fact that he'd lose her forever if he didn't do something. What mattered was that he have her back in his arms, in his life, again.

With the realization that nothing mattered as much as Star, he became aware of a sweet feeling of peace, an easing of the weight around his heart. Suddenly, life was full of possibilities, provided he could convince her to give him another chance.

The question was whether he deserved her, whether he dared take the chance to find out. Answers that had deluded him only days ago now seemed clear.

Star loved him. And he loved her. Of course he loved her. The fact had been staring him in the face for weeks. He'd been too stubborn to admit it. He loved the tilt of her chin when she was angry. He loved her humor and her wit, her intelligence and her courage. He loved the way she melted into his arms. He loved everything about her.

Together they could make something good.

In her, he'd found what had been missing in his own life. The love that comes from knowing another's heart as well as he knew his own. The love that keeps you going when all else has failed. The love that gives meaning to the quiet moments and emotion to others.

There'd been both, he recalled. Meaning. And emotion. And so much more. Why hadn't he understood that before? And why, now, when it might be too late, did he finally come to his senses? He only prayed he could find the words to tell her what was in his heart.

Fool. The word, along with a couple of other choice ones, reverberated through his mind. He didn't deserve a second chance. He had been a fool, a fact Casey had seen fit to remind him of several times a day.

Love changed a man.

After finding love with a woman like Star, everything else took second place. Including his pride. It was time he started acting on that newfound knowledge. He'd find her, make her understand that he loved her.

Together they could make something good. The actress and the rancher, he thought, and grinned. Life would never be boring.

He showered, dressed in his one good suit, and threw a couple of shirts into a bag. He found Casey in the barn.

Casey took one look at him and gave a low whistle. "Ain't you looking fine? Bring the pretty lady home."

His face creased in a rare smile. "Tell her we'll have us a wedding that'll do her proud."

Rafe thought of Casey's use of the word *home*. Lately, he'd begun to think of *home* as wherever Star was. He prayed she felt the same.

He made the trip to LA on the red-eye. It should have left him exhausted. Instead, he was pumped. He needed to find Star, see if she still felt for him what he did for her. And if she didn't? He didn't allow himself to think beyond finding her, making her listen.

He wasn't particularly surprised to find that her address wasn't listed. A star of Star's caliber would need to protect her privacy. He bought a fan magazine from a newsstand. Star's likeness stared back at him.

The picture didn't do her justice. Still, it managed to capture the vibrancy in her eyes, the jut of her chin that said she'd make the best of whatever life handed her.

It was the man accompanying her who caused him to frown. The pretty-boy good looks rubbed him the wrong way with the orthodontically straight teeth and salon tan. Rafe ran his tongue over his own teeth. Perfect, they weren't, not with the space between the front teeth and the crooked eye tooth there'd never been enough money to fix.

Was he too late? Had he come all this way to only admit defeat? His gut clenched at the word. He was far from ready to accept anything but success. He'd convince Star by whatever means necessary that he was the man for her. He'd made a poor job of it so far, but he was back on track now.

He found the studio, finagled his way past security, and located the set where he was told Star was filming. The set was a series of narrow passages and chopped-up spaces that made him think of a rabbit warren.

Everyone appeared to have a job to do. How did anyone think with the constant barrage of noises chipping away at nerves?

He cornered a kid with triple-pierced ears and blue hair who looked like she ought to be in high school. "Star Whitney. Where is she?"

"Miss Whitney?" The girl, who also sported a diamond stud in one nostril, gestured to the back. "She ought to be coming out in a couple of minutes."

He hadn't come all this way to wait another minute, another second. He started in the direction the girl had indicated when he saw her. The wave of love that roared through him was a punch to the gut. He didn't move, couldn't seem to make his legs work.

He looked more closely, saw the nerves she tried to conceal. The idea soothed his own.

The truth couldn't hide when he looked with the heart. He loved her. He had almost from the beginning. How was he to have known she'd come to mean everything to him?

She was beautiful. Yet there was a sadness to her, a shadow to her eyes that spoke of pain, and loss. In the next moment, it took on the texture of grief.

His fault.

He locked away the guilt. There'd be time, later, to indulge it. Too much time if Star turned him away. He knew the moment she spotted him. The unguarded love in her eyes was balm to his soul. It uncurled the fist around his heart, and he felt the first tingle of relief. He took a full and almost easy breath.

He'd almost thrown away everything with his pig-headedness and pride. Don't let it be too late, he prayed silently. He looked at her with such love, he was surprised she didn't feel the warmth of his gaze.

He slowed his pace as he neared her. Her scent reached him, something flowery with a hint of the sultry.

Star watched as he made his way toward her, his ground-eating strides more suitable to the open spaces of the prairie than to the crowded studio.

She was terrified. Though she'd yearned to see him again, now that he was here, she was, quite simply, terrified. Marching alongside the fear, though, was a strong dose of pride.

It was that that stiffened her backbone. She kept her eyes dry and her chin high. No way would he see what effect he had on her.

He moved with that quiet animal grace that never failed to evoke a response within her. As it did now. Even with the whole crew watching, she couldn't take her eyes from him. Production workers, grips and gaffers, lighting and sound technicians, automatically cleared the way.

Longing surged through her, sharp and painful, as her heart did a slow roll. Then she remembered. He didn't want her. That didn't keep her from loving him.

The dark jacket molding his shoulders and well-tailored trousers suited him. A white shirt contrasted sharply with his tanned face. Even if he'd been dressed in denim and leather, he would dominate the room, managing to make everything and everyone around him appear insipid by comparison.

She wasn't the only woman who noticed. His rangy body attracted feminine interest wherever he went, but it was his eyes that held her attention.

They never left her face. Not as he strode toward her, his long legs making short work of the distance between them. Not as he ignored all those who stared at him, mouths agape. Not as he made her all too aware that her feelings for him hadn't changed. Would never change.

She resisted the urge to take a step backward. Instead, she held her ground. The air quivered between them.

When he was but a scant foot from her, he stopped, legs spread in a showdown stance, hands planted on his hips. "We've got some talking to do."

She mimicked his pose, hands fisted on her hips. "As I recall, you didn't think we had anything more to say to each other."

He answered that by gently drawing her to her toes and pressing his lips to hers.

The kiss was everything she'd dreamed of for the last month. She gave herself up to it, savoring every sound, every touch, every texture. His jaw against her cheek. The strength of his arms as they closed around her.

A sigh of contentment rippled from her as she melted further into his embrace, and the tightness she'd carried in her chest broke apart.

"We have to talk."

"I don't have—"

"You don't have to say a thing. All you have to do is listen."

She huffed out a breath and remembered the onlookers. "My dressing room." She led the way to the room assigned to her, slammed the door behind them, and snicked the lock in place.

He eyed the mange of yellow fur stretched out on a cot. "What's that?"

"Bailey."

"What's a Bailey?"

"It's a cat," Star said with a glance at the animal who now began to clean its tail with slurping licks.

Rafe pulled out the bag he'd brought with him. "I brought you something."

She looked inside. Her lips twitched in a reluctant smile. A boot. "Just one?" She refused to let loose the laugh that bubbled inside her.

"I ate the other one. I was wrong about you. I was wrong about a lot of things." The words didn't stick in his throat as he'd feared. They felt right. More, he felt right with the rapid beat of his heart mingling with hers.

"You bothered me. From the beginning. I looked at you and saw a woman I could love, though I hadn't figured that out."

"You didn't like me."

"I didn't *want* to like you. Big difference. Why didn't you tell me who you were?"

"When I realized you didn't know, it seemed easier to leave it that way. I liked being just Star Whitney. I worked hard to get where I am. I liked the money, the fame. But after a while, it wasn't enough. I didn't know what I was missing . . . until I met you."

He hadn't known he was holding his breath until it expelled in a rush of air. He tried a smile, thought he saw the trace of one in return. It made him decide to give her the rest of it. The muscles necessary for a smile felt rusty from disuse.

He thought he heard his jaw crack with the effort and didn't care. Smiling felt too good.

"I couldn't find my balance. I couldn't find my balance without you. And then I stood in the studio and saw you. There she is, I thought, so my life's as it should be."

She wouldn't fade into the background. He remembered his frantic rush to see her, his impatience when he couldn't find her. "You know the worst of me, but you still manage to love me." He prayed that was true.

"What I feel for you, what you make me feel, is the best of me. You make me want to take another chance."

"What kind of chance?"

"On love."

She raised her gaze to his and saw what she'd nearly given up hoping to find there. Love. Her heart rolled over in her chest, the most lovely sensation she'd ever known.

She pressed a hand there, as though to push out air. She couldn't find any. She told herself to breathe, but breathing seemed incidental to rejoicing.

Rafe framed her face in his hands. "I want you in every way a man can want a woman. You are my heartsong."

"Heartsong?"

"That's what the Cheyenne call it." He took her hand and placed it on his heart. "I carry you here. Whether we're together or apart."

The idea touched her, but not as much as the tenderness in his voice. "And you are mine."

"I love you. With everything I am. Body, mind, heart. When we're in our nineties, I'll still need you. Still want you. Still love you." The declaration was as blunt and honest as everything else about him. And just as impossible to resist.

It was a shock to feel the scrape of tears in her throat, an effort to swallow them back.

Before she could do so, he slid a hand up to cup the

back of her neck, to massage away the tension. "You never have to be alone again. If you'll have me."

And her heart simply shattered.

"There's something I have to do." He dropped to one knee and took her hand in his. "Estrella Whitney, will you marry me?" He didn't give her time to answer as he went on in a rush of words, "I've got no right asking, but—"

She linked fingers with the hand that held hers, felt the promise in them. "Did you mean what you said? That you loved me?"

"You know I do."

"Then you have every right."

He stood, then cupped her shoulders, bringing her close enough that she could feel the thump of his heart against hers. "I have only to look at you and the world comes to me. You are my life."

"You are everything I want, everything I need."

His gaze settled on her with a warmth that belied the blast of air conditioning inside the studio. "I'll make you happy. I swear it."

"You already have."

His lips covered hers in a kiss so sweet, so tender, that tears filled her eyes. When he lifted his head and stared at her with those oh-so-dark eyes, she knew a fulfillment denied her over the last month.

"I was running scared," he said at last. "I talked myself into believing I was doing it for you. I didn't want to trap you."

"Idiot." But the word was said softly.

He took courage from the love that shone in her eyes. "I love you, my Estrella." He couldn't say the words enough. "I want you in my life. Anyway I can get you. If it means living in LA for part of the year, we'll work it out. We'll make it work."

"Acting is what I do. It's not what I am. Or who I am."

"I'm starting to see that."

"It took you long enough."

His lips stretched into a smile. "Yeah. I'm a slow learner. I'll need a good teacher."

A matching smile tweaked the corners of her lips. "A teacher, huh?"

"It'd be a lifetime job." His gaze searched hers. "I've always been partial to the idea of a wedding at the ranch."

"I'd like that." She could see it now. Herself in a long white gown, carrying a bouquet of wildflowers. The picture, so vivid, took on details. Rafe would be more handsome than ever in a dark suit and snowy white shirt.

They'd have the wedding at his house, make it a family affair with just a few close friends present. Following the ceremony, there'd be a party. His friends and hers.

"I can't promise it'll be the fanciest wedding there ever was, but we'll do it up any way you want. The ladies in town will most likely want to help."

Her lips curved at the idea. No, it wasn't the

Hollywood match everyone assumed she would some-day make. Nor would she have the glamorous wedding that accompanied such unions.

Thank heaven.

It would be a love match and a family wedding. "All I want is you." She lifted his hand to her lips and pressed a kiss to his palm. "When we're married, I can help."

His lips kicked up at the corners. "You gonna learn how to drive a tractor?"

She poked him in the arm. "I mean really help. I've got some ideas . . ."

He kissed her.

Gently.

Tenderly.

Imprinting the shape and texture of his mouth on her own.

So exquisite was the moment, that tears crowded her eyes, spilled over to stream down her cheeks.

Gently, Rafe wiped away the tears with the pads of his thumbs. "You always manage to surprise me, my Star."

She looped her arms around his neck, let both heart and mind go. "I can't promise to do that," she said, "but I can promise to love you." She placed her lips on his. "Always."

Epilogue

"Why isn't your name on the program?" Rafe asked after scanning the printed program listing everyone from the stars of the play to the lighting and sound technicians.

"Mine is an advisory capacity only," Star said primly. "The group has a lot of talent. I barely did anything."

He grunted. He knew Star had spent every minute she could squeeze from her already full schedule coaching the young actors.

Today's performance was a special one. Shyly, she'd told him about her work with autistic children and how she'd arranged for the kids to attend the matinee.

The small children sat quietly. Rafe divided his attention between watching them and watching the actors.

The story unfolded. Despite having seen the play several times, Rafe found himself spellbound. He applauded enthusiastically as the curtain came down for the final time.

"Mith Whitney," Tommy, the most vocal of the children said. "I . . . I . . . I liked it."

Star knelt to hug him. "I'm glad."

He hugged her back.

Rafe felt his heart turn over, making him fall in love with her all over again. "I wonder if you know how much I love you."

She smiled up at him. "I know."

And that, he thought, was the greatest wonder of all.